"You coul... man," she whispered.

His smile fled. "I'd never hurt you, my love."

Misty knew he could hurt her a great deal. Yet suddenly it didn't matter. She'd played it safe all her life, but no more. This man was everything she'd always dreamed of. He could bring her untold bliss. And if heaven came with a price tag, well, so be it.

She stood on tiptoe, and when Brandon's mouth closed over hers, she was the one who deepened the kiss. He made a sound of pleasure, but when she pushed his robe open so she could caress his bare chest, he stiffened.

His hand closed over hers like a vise. "You're playing with fire, little one," he warned.

She laughed softly. "You do seem rather warm."

His eyes narrowed. "I never figured you for a tease."

She put her arms around his neck and tilted her head to gaze up at him. "For an experienced man, you're awfully dense."

He scanned her dreamy face with dawning excitement. "You mean—"

"Do I have to *ask* you to make love to me?"

Dear Reader,

Each and every month, to satisfy your taste for substantial, memorable, emotion-packed stories of life and love, of dreams and possibilities, Silhouette brings you six extremely *Special Editions*.

This month, to mark our continually renewed commitment to bring you the very best and the brightest in contemporary romance writing, Silhouette *Special Edition* features a distinguished lineup of authors you've chosen as your favorites. Nora Roberts, Linda Howard, Tracy Sinclair, Curtiss Ann Matlock, Jo Ann Algermissen and Emilie Richards each deliver a powerful new romantic novel, along with a personal message to you, the reader.

Keep a sharp eye out for all six—you won't want to miss this dazzling constellation of romance stars. And stay with us in the months to come, because each and every month, Silhouette *Special Edition* is dedicated to becoming more special than ever.

From all the authors and editors of *Special Edition*, Warmest wishes,

Leslie Kazanjian
Senior Editor

TRACY SINCLAIR
More Precious Than Jewels

Silhouette Special Edition

Published by Silhouette Books New York

America's Publisher of Contemporary Romance

SILHOUETTE BOOKS
300 East 42nd St., New York, N.Y. 10017

ISBN: 0-373-09453-1

First Silhouette Books printing May 1988
Second printing May 1988

Printed in the U.S.A.

Books by Tracy Sinclair

Author of more than twenty Silhouette novels, **TRACY SINCLAIR** also contributes to various magazines and newspapers. She says her years as a photojournalist provided the most exciting adventures—and misadventures—of her life. An extensive traveler—from Alaska to South America, and most places in between—and a dedicated volunteer worker—from suicide-prevention programs to English-as-a-second-language lessons—the California resident has accumulated countless fascinating experiences, settings and acquaintances to draw on in plotting her romances.

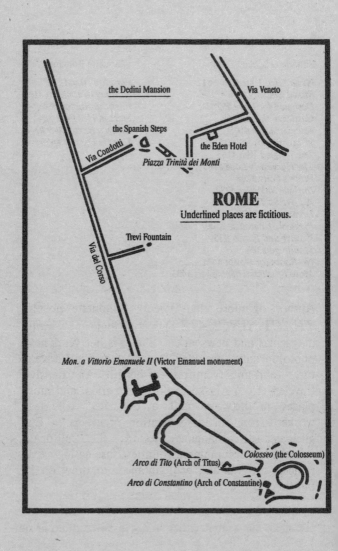

the Dedini Mansion

Via Veneto

the Spanish Steps

Via Condotti

the Eden Hotel

Piazza Trinità dei Monti

ROME
Underlined places are fictitious.

Trevi Fountain

Via del Corso

Mon. a Vittorio Emanuele II (Victor Emanuel monument)

Arco di Tito (Arch of Titus)

Colosseo (the Colosseum)

Arco di Constantino (Arch of Constantine)

Chapter One

The torrent of rain pounding against Misty Carlysle's window added to her gloom. The darkness outside didn't help, either, nor did the wind moaning around her apartment building. She could hear it even over the traffic in the slick street below.

When the phone rang she was tempted not to answer it, but she knew wallowing in misery wouldn't solve anything.

"What took you so long?" her aunt's voice greeted her. "I was about to hang up. I thought you weren't home."

"Sophia!" Misty exclaimed in delight. "Where are you?"

The question wasn't an idle one. Countess Sophia Elaine Grayson de Blessard could be phoning from anyplace on the globe, or at least any of the fancier spots. She spent her winters either skiing in Switzerland or sunning herself on the Riviera. The other seasons were spent in equally fashionable locales.

"I'm right here in New York, pet," Sophia answered. "At least for a few days."

"Will I get to see you?" Misty asked.

"Of course! Would I miss a chance to see my favorite niece?"

Misty smiled. "I'm your only niece," she pointed out.

"You'd still be my favorite, darling. How soon can you get over here? I'm at the Plaza."

"I'll leave right now."

The sparkle was back in Misty's violet eyes as she ran a comb through her glossy black hair and touched up her lipstick. Even the daunting prospect of getting a cab in New York City on a rainy night couldn't dampen her excitement. Just the sound of her aunt's voice raised her flagging spirits.

Sophia had that effect on people. She made even the dullest ones feel charming and witty.

Although she was in her mid-forties now, Sophia still had the unquenchable thirst for life that had led her to reject the comfortable existence most people settled for. Instead, she went out in the world seeking adventure. What she found was a fairy-tale life.

After graduating from college as a language major, she had landed a job with the American Embassy in Paris. That provided entrée into Parisian high society. She was wined and dined in the continental manner by scores of fascinating men, many of whom proposed marriage.

Sophia had tactfully rejected all of them. She was having much too good a time to tie herself down to one man—until she met Lucien de Blessard, Compte de Tremaine. It was love at first sight for both of them. They married after a whirlwind courtship and lived a life of glamour and luxury.

Sophia was utterly devastated when Lucien was tragically killed in a racing-car accident. She resumed her old life eventually, but she had never remarried.

Misty hadn't seen her aunt in over a year, and their reunion in Sophia's flower-filled suite was joyous.

"Let me look at you!" After an initial hug, Sophia held Misty at arm's length.

She scanned her niece's thickly fringed, violet-colored eyes, her slightly tilted nose and generous mouth, and the cloud of raven hair that made her flawless skin look like fine porcelain.

"You're as gorgeous as ever," Sophia proclaimed.

"You're the one who's gorgeous." Misty's eyes were filled with admiration as she looked at the older woman's unlined face framed by a chic hairdo. "You never get a day older."

"Age is a state of mind." Sophia dismissed the subject as uninteresting. "Sit down and tell me every single thing that's happened since I saw you last."

Misty's smile was rueful. "That should take about five minutes."

Sophia's eyebrows rose. "As bad as that?"

"No, I was just joking. I meant in comparison to your exciting life." Misty was determined not to air her troubles. This was a happy occasion. "Tell me what you've been doing so I can live vicariously."

"You should be living your own life," her aunt scolded.

"It couldn't compare to yours. I want to hear about exotic places and glamorous parties crammed with fancy titles and celebrities."

"I did go to a fabulous ball recently," Sophia admitted. "It was given by that millionaire from Argentina. Just between us, darling, I wouldn't inquire too closely into how he made his money, but the party was fantastic. Would you believe four orchestras and a veritable jungle of orchids flown in from the tropics? The guests came by private jets from all over the world. But wait until I tell you what happened when this weird rock star showed up."

Sophia had an endless supply of stories, all entertaining, but they were interrupted often. The telephone rang constantly. Sophia had friends everywhere, and they were all eager to see her.

She returned after finishing with the latest caller and said, "Enough about me. I haven't even asked about your parents yet. Is Claire still president of the garden club and everything else that's trivial in Darien?"

Misty's mother was Sophia's older sister. The two had nothing in common, not even appearance. In a family of tall, dark, reserved people, Sophia was small, blond and vivacious.

Misty had always adored her aunt, but she'd had to walk a fine line between her mother's disapproval of her sibling and her aunt's impatience with *hers*. The sisters loved each other in their own way, but neither approved of the other.

"Mother and Dad are fine." Misty's tone was neutral. "I'm sure she'd love to hear from you while you're here."

"Of course I'll call her." Sophia sighed. "She'll probably feel honor bound to come in and have lunch with me. You will join us, won't you? We need a moderator—or perhaps I should say a referee."

"I don't understand how you can get along with the most temperamental people in the world, but not your own sister," Misty remarked in mild frustration.

"I'm really terribly fond of her. It's just that Claire is so... *practical*!"

Misty grinned. "How can you say that about a woman who named her baby Mistinguette? I've been keeping it a dark secret all my life."

"It's too bad that streak of romance turned into conformity."

Misty shrugged. "She's happy."

An unconscious inflection in her voice made Sophia look more closely at her. "You're undoubtedly right. How about you?" She asked the question casually. "Still working in the same office?"

"No, I... not anymore."

The noncommittal answer indicated Misty didn't wish to pursue the subject, but that didn't deter her aunt. "Where are you working now?"

"Well, actually... I'll be looking for another job. I quit mine this afternoon."

Sophia assessed her niece's grim expression. "Sometimes a change is beneficial. It must have been boring working in that stuffy law office."

"No, it was fascinating! Each case was different. I got to sit in on a lot of the strategy meetings and see how they were going to be handled."

"Then why did you quit?" Sophia asked quietly.

"Oh, well..." Misty realized her enthusiasm had betrayed her. She stood up and thrust her hands into the pockets of her jeans. "It was time to move on."

"You always used to confide in me," Sophia reminded her gently. "Have I changed in some way?"

"It isn't that. I guess I didn't want anything to spoil our visit. It's so great seeing you again."

"Why don't we get whatever's bothering you out of the way, and then we can go back to enjoying ourselves."

Misty sighed. "It isn't anything earth-shattering. One of the attorneys in the office is a complete jerk. He's been coming on to me for months. I tried everything I could to discourage him, but he has the sensitivity of an orangutan. I just got tired of the situation. Everything came to a head today. I told him off and quit."

"You didn't have to put up with that. He subjected you to sexual harassment!" Sophia exclaimed. "You could bring charges."

"He's married," Misty said succinctly.

Sophia's mouth curled in disgust. "His kind is *always* married. What does that have to do with it?"

"I know his wife. She's young and naïve—and eight months pregnant. I just couldn't bring that kind of misery on her now."

"I see your point," Sophia admitted. "But you can't let him get away with something like this. You have to expose him for the sake of all the women who will come after you."

"I think he'll be on his good behavior, for a while anyway." Misty smiled in remembered satisfaction. "Mr. Leffcourt, the senior partner, called me into his office when he heard I was quitting. He asked why, and I told him Mitchell expected more of me than I was willing to give."

"I'd have spoken a little plainer than that."

"Mr. Leffcourt got the message. He offered to assign me to one of the other attorneys."

"That wasn't acceptable? I thought you liked what you were doing."

"I did. At least I thought so." Misty moved to the elegantly draped window and looked moodily out at the darkened park. "Sometimes I feel as though I'm just spinning my wheels. What have I really accomplished?"

"You must be an excellent legal secretary if the senior partner of a prestigious firm didn't want to lose you."

"I'm good at what I do," Misty answered without conceit. "I won't have any trouble getting another position. But is that all there is? I'm twenty-six years old, and life seems to be passing me by."

"Then do something about it! Leaving your job was the right decision. There's a whole world out there. Reach for it!"

Misty turned back to the brightly lit room, trying to shake off her discouragement. She mustered a smile. "Okay, I'll think positively. My next boss will be a courtly old gentleman who never makes a pass and gives automatic raises."

"Is that your idea of positive thinking?" Sophia asked disgustedly. "How about your personal life? What do you intend to do about that?"

"There's nothing wrong with it," Misty mumbled.

Sophia gazed at her niece's striking face and lovely figure. Even jeans topped by a baggy sweater couldn't detract from Misty's curved body and long legs. She was exceptionally beautiful. The only thing missing was the soft glow of a woman in love.

"What about men? I haven't heard you mention anyone in particular."

"There's no one special at the moment, but I go out on dates."

"With earnest young attorneys and law clerks, no doubt," Sophia remarked dryly.

"What's wrong with that? We have a lot in common," Misty answered defensively.

"It sounds as exciting as watching television with one's brother. You should be riding to the hounds in England with a handsome duke, or joining a house party at the villa of some Italian noble."

Misty smiled. "I'm willing. The trouble is that I haven't had an invitation to do any of those things lately."

Sophia stared at her thoughtfully. "No, but you're going to."

Misty looked faintly alarmed. "If you're thinking of arranging a blind date for me, forget it. I appreciate your concern, but I'd be hopelessly out of my depth with your high-rolling friends."

"Don't be ridiculous! All you need are some adequate clothes."

"Please don't pressure anyone into calling me," Misty pleaded. "It would only be a disaster."

"Relax, pet. I agree that blind dates are barbaric. I'm going to launch you into society myself."

"I thought you were leaving in a few days. Wouldn't it be more of a shove than a launch?"

"I *am* leaving, but you'll be coming with me."

Misty's first reaction was delight, followed closely by second thoughts. "I don't think this is the right time for a vacation—now that I'm out of work."

"What better time? You won't have to worry about getting back by a certain date. We can wander around Europe, wherever anything interesting is happening."

"It sounds fabulous," Misty agreed wistfully. "But dream vacations aren't for the unemployed."

"Who needs one more? Don't argue with me. It's all settled. We leave for Rome in three days."

"I really shouldn't spend all my savings," Misty said hesitantly.

"This is my treat," Sophia informed her.

"I couldn't let you do that," Misty protested.

"Consider it your birthday and Christmas presents combined."

"You can't afford it, Sophia," Misty said quietly.

She was one of the few people who knew the truth of that statement. Everyone simply assumed Sophia was wealthy. She certainly lived like a rich woman. Lucien's affairs, however, had been left in a tangled mess.

He had excelled at many things. Unfortunately, high finance wasn't one of them. He'd gone through most of his inherited wealth, cushioned from reality by a naïve belief that his money was inexhaustible.

After her husband's tragic death Sophia continued her flamboyant life-style, but not entirely through self-indulgence. In large part it was to protect Lucien's image. She didn't want anyone to know that he hadn't provided for her handsomely.

One thing he'd left her was magnificent jewelry. Through the years she'd sold it whenever the need arose and replaced each piece with an excellent copy.

"Money is to spend," Sophia stated firmly, dismissing Misty's objection to her offer.

"You must be running out of yours about now."

Sophia shrugged. "I'll worry about that when the time comes."

"What will you do?" Misty asked soberly.

"Any number of things. I can become a decorator, or a party consultant, or go to work for a couturier. It will be a whole new adventure."

"Have you ever considered marrying again?" Misty asked tentatively.

Sophia's gaiety disappeared. "That's not something you do for money."

Misty gazed with admiration at the indomitable older woman. She never let despair get the upper hand. "I wish I could be more like you."

Sophia laughed, her sense of fun restored. "You can, darling. Just cut your hair and dye it blond."

"I would if I thought it would do the trick."

"I know of an easier way. Come to Rome with me. It will be an adventure you'll never forget."

Misty made up her mind in a lightning turnaround. Why not? What was there to keep her here? The time had come to stop being so conservative. Just once she wanted to do something without weighing all the pros and cons. Sophia was right. The world was a great big apple, and she was going to take a bite instead of a nibble!

"I'll do it! I'll go with you."

"You won't regret it," Sophia said approvingly. "I guarantee this trip will change your whole life."

The plane ride from New York was Misty's entry into the world of luxury she was about to inhabit. The first-class section was small but roomy, with several flight attendants to provide instant service for the relatively few passengers.

They were offered lobster and caviar canapés on fine china, and roast beef served from a heated cart, the way it often was in a fine restaurant. After watching a movie, Misty discovered that her seat reclined until it was almost like a bed. She had a long nap and arrived in Rome well rested.

The Eden Hotel was evidently a favorite of Sophia's. She was greeted with much fanfare and fond recollections of previous visits. They were shown to their suite by the manager, who had remembered the things that pleased her: flowers in all the rooms, a bottle of champagne cooling in a silver ice bucket, and perfumed shampoo in the bathrooms.

Misty felt delightfully continental as she sipped champagne while unpacking.

When they met in the living room afterward, Sophia said, "Would you like to go down to the dining room or have something sent up here?"

Misty looked at her watch. "Is it dinnertime? My watch says three o'clock. Is that morning or afternoon? I'm all turned around."

"Don't think about it. When in Rome, do as the Romans do."

"Okay, then let's go see some of them."

"The dining room it is. We'll have to change clothes."

"What should I wear?" Misty asked.

"Something smashing. You never know who you'll meet."

Misty's mouth turned down ruefully. "My wardrobe can best be described as utilitarian."

"That's something we'll have to remedy tomorrow. It's too bad we couldn't have stopped off in Paris, but the Italians have some elegant couturiers, too."

"I will *not* let you spend a fortune for clothes I won't even be able to wear when I go home."

"You just got here. Why worry about what's going to happen when you go home?"

Misty decided there was no sense in arguing about it at that point. Why spoil their first evening in one of the most exciting cities of the world?

She was looking over her decidedly uninteresting wardrobe when Sophia joined her, carrying something glittery over one arm.

"You're too tall to wear most of my things, but this top would fit you." She held out a wisp of silk chiffon embroidered with crystal and silver beads in an intricate design. "It will look stunning with black satin pants."

Misty held it against herself and looked in the mirror. "It's gorgeous! I don't have satin pants, though. Will a black skirt do?"

"I suppose it will have to." Sophia glanced disparagingly at the contents of the open closet. "We'll have to make more than one shopping excursion, I see."

"You're darling to lend me this," Misty said hastily to distract her. "I'll be very careful."

"It's yours if you like. I never cared much for it—too *jeune fille.*"

Misty knew that wasn't so when she put on the beaded top. It was the height of sophistication. The neckline plunged daringly, and the crystal beads sparkled like diamonds. The narrow black skirt she was forced to substitute proved an adequate alternative to pants. Misty felt glamorous and desirable.

Her mouth curved in self-mockery as she swung her long black hair aside to fasten dangling earrings to her lobes. "Too bad there's no one who's panting after me," she told her mirror image.

"You look divine!" Sophia exclaimed when she saw her.

"You're pretty terrific looking yourself."

Sophia wore a simple black dress that was a perfect foil for the magnificent sapphire-and-diamond necklace that circled her throat. A matching bracelet adorned one wrist.

Misty's eyes widened. "Are those jewels real?"

Her aunt smiled mischievously. "If you can't tell, darling, what difference does it make?"

Misty's private doubts about being overdressed were laid to rest when they entered the dining room. The tables were filled with elegantly gowned women, and men in dark suits. A few even wore dinner jackets.

The maître d' was absent from his post, so they had to wait a few moments to be seated. Sophia used the time to scan the room for acquaintances. Her idle glance suddenly sharpened as it rested on a man dining alone.

"I think we struck gold on our first try," she murmured. "I'll bet he's an Italian prince, or a count at the very least. Isn't he the ultimate?"

After following her aunt's gaze, Misty had to agree. The man appeared to be in his mid-thirties. His face was not only handsome, it was rugged as well. Good bone structure gave him a strong jaw and high cheekbones. His straight nose was classic, and his dark hair was cut faultlessly. A deep tan accentuated light eyes.

"Aren't his eyes unusual?" Misty whispered. "I wonder what color they are."

"We'll find out," Sophia answered.

"You're not going to do anything outrageous?" Misty asked in alarm.

"Trust me, pet." The maître d' arrived and started to lead them to a table, but Sophia said, "I'd prefer that one." She indicated a table near the lone diner.

"As you wish, madame."

Misty followed them with a feeling of apprehension that was justified. Their path led past the unknown man's table. As Sophia drew abreast of him she stumbled—something Misty had never seen her do in her entire life. She jostled the man's arm as he was raising a glass of water to his lips. A little of it splashed on his immaculate, custom-made shirt.

"Oh, I'm so *terribly* sorry!" Sophia gasped. "Can you forgive me?"

"That's quite all right. Accidents do happen." He stood up, dabbing at his shirtfront.

"You're American!" Sophia's gasp was genuine this time.

Even, white teeth gleamed in his tanned face. "We do get around, don't we?"

"I'll bring you another napkin, sir," the maître d' said.

"No problem." The man's amused eyes discovered Misty. His expression changed to male appreciation. "Enjoy your dinner," he said graciously.

"I could have sworn he was Italian," Sophia said after they were seated. "But that was before I saw those marvelous green eyes. Did you ever see such an unusual color? And those broad shoulders and slim hips—the man's a positive Adonis!"

"How could you have bumped into him like that?" Misty demanded. "He knew you did it on purpose. I was never so mortified in my life!"

"I don't know what you're talking about," Sophia replied innocently. "I could scarcely help it if I tripped. He was quite nice about it, I thought."

"Let's order," Misty said grimly as the waiter presented large tasseled menus.

"Order me an aperitif, darling. I'll decide on dinner when I return." Sophia stood up. "I have to visit the powder room."

"We just came down from the suite!" Misty protested.

"When nature calls, one answers."

Misty watched her aunt thread her way toward the exit. To her relief, Sophia didn't choose the path past the good-looking man's table.

Misty inspected him through long lashes while pretending to scan the menu. She wasn't the only one, either. He was the kind of man who attracted attention, but it didn't ruffle his poise. Although he couldn't help noticing the glances cast his way, he seemed completely at ease.

What was a man like that doing alone? Misty wondered. She was so busy speculating about him that she didn't notice her aunt hand a note to the headwaiter.

"Have you decided what you're going to have?" Sophia reappeared a short time later. "Everything is superb here, especially the *piccata di vitello*—what we call veal piccata."

"That sounds good," Misty answered absently.

She was watching a waiter approach the man's table and offer a bottle of wine for his inspection. They had a short conversation after which the man glanced over at their table, looking at Misty with a rather sardonic expression. Her cheeks warmed at being caught staring, and she turned away hurriedly.

"I can't believe there's no one here I know," Sophia was saying. "Perhaps there's a party somewhere."

"Surely you'd be invited if there were," Misty teased.

"I might have been. I haven't looked at my engagement book since I left for New York. The only date I remember is the Dedinis' Scarlet Ball on the twentieth."

"I presume all the women are supposed to wear red, not just a scarlet letter on their chests."

"Right the first time, although your second guess might be more apt in some cases," Sophia answered dryly. "You'll adore the Dedini villa. It's filled with priceless antiques. The Count is an industrialist and frightfully rich."

"It all sounds very grand, but I haven't been invited."

"You will be when I tell them you're my niece."

"You mustn't feel responsible for me," Misty objected. "It's enough just to be here."

Before Sophia could answer, the man she'd bumped into appeared at their table carrying a bottle of wine. "This was very thoughtful of you, but completely unnecessary," he said.

"I wanted to make amends for my clumsiness." Sophia's explanation was given demurely, but her eyes inspected him with lively interest.

"You could never be anything except graceful." His smile held a hint of mockery. "But it would give me great pleasure if you'd share this with me." He held up the bottle.

"What a lovely idea!" Sophia exclaimed. "By all means, do join us."

Misty's cheeks burned with renewed embarrassment when she realized what her aunt had done. Regardless of how elegantly it had been engineered, Sophia had picked up this man! And he knew it. That accounted for the derisive look on his face when he'd glanced over at them. He probably thought Misty was a coconspirator.

She couldn't look at him as he told Sophia his name was Brandon Powers. But she had to glance up when her aunt introduced her.

"Misty. What a lovely name," he remarked in a husky voice that sent tingles down her spine.

She gazed into eyes that were like emeralds, hard on the surface but with hidden fire. In a fleeting flash of intuition Misty sensed something out of kilter, a primitive drive that was at odds with his urbane manner. She stared at him, unable to think of anything to say.

Sophia was never bothered by that affliction. She had developed the social graces into a fine art. To start with, she established a first-name basis among the three of them, then proceeded from there.

"Have you been in Rome long?" She made the query sound like pleasant interest instead of the quest for information Misty knew she was on.

"Just a few days, although I've been in Europe for several weeks," he answered.

Sophia clicked her tongue. "I do hope we haven't met at the end of your vacation."

"No, fortunately for me. Actually I'm on a temporarily permanent vacation."

"That sounds intriguing. You really must explain."

Brandon laughed. "It's quite simple. I made such a nuisance of myself in the family banking business that the board of directors decided I should take an extended leave of absence—as far away from Philadelphia as possible."

"How terribly clever of you!" Sophia exclaimed.

"It wasn't planned. I simply have an underdeveloped business sense. If it were up to me, I'd approve loans for yachts and private islands in the Pacific, not just things like twenty-year mortgages."

Sophia nodded approvingly. "I agree with you wholeheartedly. Everyone is entitled to his or her dream."

Misty listened with growing disappointment. Brandon Powers was nothing but a dilettante, a rich man's son with no sense of responsibility. The kind who drifted through life looking only for amusement.

So much for her feeling that he was different somehow, a renaissance man who wouldn't be deterred by obstacles or danger. What she'd taken for confidence in his own ability was merely the assurance that unlimited money can bring.

He turned to her, trying to draw her out. "What's your dream, Misty? Perhaps I can arrange it."

"I doubt it," she answered coolly. "I wouldn't know what to do with a yacht. My tastes are simple."

His gaze swept over her expensive beaded top. "If you say so," he murmured.

She wanted to correct the mistaken impression her borrowed finery had given, but it didn't seem worthwhile. They'd never see each other again once dinner was over.

Misty had reckoned without Sophia, however.

"My niece is dreadfully conservative," her aunt said. "It took all my powers of persuasion to get her to Rome."

"I'm glad you succeeded." He made the polite comment sound sincere.

Brandon turned his full attention on Misty, looking at her with the awareness of a man for a beautiful woman. He gave the impression of wanting to be alone with her, someplace intimate.

The effect was potent. Even though she knew it was an act he put on for every female, a little thrill of anticipation tightened Misty's nerves. She could almost believe they were on the brink of a relationship filled with excitement.

"I promised her the time of her life," Sophia was saying.

"Could I volunteer to contribute to the effort?" Something flickered deep in his eyes.

Misty pulled herself up sharply. Brandon's expertise had made her forget for a moment how shallow he was, but it wouldn't happen again.

"I believe you and my aunt have more in common," she said crisply.

Sophia made a small sound of annoyance, but Brandon was amused rather than insulted. "My invitation was meant for both of you. Would you be my guests at La Paloma? It's one of the 'in' nightclubs in Rome."

"You would know," Misty muttered under her breath.

Sophia frowned at her disapprovingly. "We'd be delighted," she told him with a smile.

Misty was tempted to tell them to go without her, but Sophia was already displeased with her. That was no way to start a dream vacation. They were going to have a long talk later, though, she vowed.

The nightclub was crowded, but they were shown immediately to a choice table after a large bill changed hands between Brandon and the captain.

"I'm glad we'll have such a splendid view of the floor show. You'll love it," Sophia told Misty.

"You've been here before?" Brandon asked.

"A month ago with one of the backers."

"Would that be Carlos Galluchi by any chance?" he asked.

"Yes! Do you know him?"

"Very well, and his sister, also."

"What a small world!" Sophia exclaimed. "Who else are you acquainted with in Rome? I'll bet we know a lot of the same people."

"Well, let's see." Most of the names he mentioned were familiar to her. He finished with the Dedinis.

"You're going to the Scarlet Ball, of course," she said.

"Isn't everyone?"

"They'll be coming from all over the continent," she agreed. "Do you by any chance know the Courtneys?"

Misty listened quietly as they discussed friends of Sophia's, many of whom he knew. The people and the places gave a picture of aimless existence.

Suddenly Sophia's eyes widened as she glanced over Brandon's shoulder. "Speak of the devil! Isn't that Alec Courtney at that big table? I must go over and say hello. He still owes me money on a bet we made at Ascot."

"Your aunt is unique." Brandon smiled at her bright head bobbing through the crowd.

"Yes, she really enjoys life." Misty sighed unconsciously. "I wish I could be more like her."

"Don't you enjoy life?"

"Oh, sure, I guess so. But mine isn't as exciting."

"I can scarcely believe that."

"It's true. I work for a living."

"That can be exciting."

Then why don't *you*? she wanted to ask, but she conquered the impulse. It was none of her business.

"What do you do?" He sounded as though he were really interested.

Misty knew he wasn't, but since he'd asked, she told him.

"If your job isn't satisfying enough, have you ever thought of being a lawyer instead of a legal secretary?"

"It takes so long," she said hesitantly. "And the market is glutted with attorneys right now."

"That's no excuse. There's always room at the top, which is where you should aim," he said forcefully.

"Why didn't you?" she asked quietly.

A curtain seemed to drop behind his eyes. He sat back in his chair and picked up his drink. "I'm a classic example of too much money and too little ambition."

"There's nothing you want to be?" she probed.

Brandon's mouth curved in a mocking smile. "I hate to fail at anything, and since my talents seemed best suited to being a playboy, that's what I became."

Misty stared at him with a slight frown. Something was very wrong here. She hadn't imagined his intensity when he was urging her to widen her horizons. He had exuded confidence and drive. Could a man like that settle for so much less for himself?

Her troubled expression didn't escape him. His voice held hidden amusement as he said, "Your aunt approves of me even if you don't."

"Sophia is a darling, but she judges people by their manners, not their morals," Misty answered without thinking.

Brandon laughed outright. "If you've been speculating about my love life, the details aren't nearly as lurid as you suspect."

Misty blushed painfully. "It was just a figure of speech. I wasn't implying...I mean..."

He took pity on her. "That's all right, honey. After meeting some of Sophia's crowd, I can see where you got the impression."

"She isn't like them," Misty said loyally. "Sophia's flighty manner is just an act. You mustn't dismiss her as another social butterfly. She works really hard for a number of charitable organizations."

Brandon chuckled. "I'll bet she's good at getting money out of people."

"She is. Everyone loves her."

"With good reason. But she shouldn't be so...trusting. Does she keep those jewels in the hotel safe?" he asked casually.

Misty knew Brandon was referring to the way Sophia had picked him up. In his case it had been harmless, but she recognized the implicit warning. He didn't know the sapphires Sophia had on that night were probably fake.

"I'm sure she's careful with her jewelry," Misty answered noncommittally.

"That's good." Brandon lost interest in the subject. "Would you like to dance?" he asked as the orchestra started to play.

The chemistry between them ignited the minute Misty moved into his arms. Her body conformed to his effortlessly, and she couldn't suppress a small sigh of contentment. His embrace tightened, but he cradled her gently, as though aware of the power of his big frame.

They danced in silence for a few moments before Brandon said, "You smell wonderful." His lips slid across her temple as he buried his face in the scented cloud of her hair. "What are you wearing?"

"It's called Divine."

"A very apt name." He lifted his head to smile down at her. "That's what I thought when I caught my first glimpse of you."

"Was that before or after you wiped the water off your shirt?" she joked.

"It was when I saw you standing in the doorway."

"You never noticed me," she protested.

"Didn't I? If fate hadn't taken a hand, I'd have found some way to meet you."

Misty's smile faded. She had to bring things out in the open. "You know it was Sophia, not fate."

"Don't be so sure. Maybe she was just an instrument. You can't discount the odds against two displaced Americans meeting in Rome, both unattached and looking for adventure. I knew immediately that you were a kindred spirit."

"Perhaps you're just homesick."

"It's possible, although that doesn't minimize your attraction."

She thought his voice had an odd note. "Do you have any plans to return to America?"

"Sometimes I wonder."

This time Misty was sure she wasn't imagining it. There was a definite tone of grimness about the short answer.

"Maybe they'd let you come home if you promised to settle down and stop financing pie-in-the-sky schemes," she said tentatively.

"That would take all the fun out of life. I like living on the cutting edge."

His smile was meant to indicate it was a joke, but something in his face told Misty he was telling the truth. Where did he find the cutting edge in his current lifestyle? The only danger was getting a bad olive in a martini.

"Besides, why would I want to go home now that you're here?" His voice was like warm honey. "We have a lot of getting acquainted to do."

Misty gazed into his handsome face, knowing he could turn charm on like a faucet. But suddenly it didn't matter. She had come to Rome looking for the color and gaiety that surrounded Sophia—and she'd found it. Brandon could supply both in great measure. It was time to accept people the way they were, as her aunt did.

Misty's smile was enchanting as she tilted her head to look up at him. "I'm glad you're staying."

"You couldn't get rid of me if you tried," he murmured huskily.

Chapter Two

Misty could have stayed in Brandon's arms for hours, but eventually the music stopped. They went back to their table to find their party greatly expanded. Sophia had returned, bringing most of the other group with her.

Brandon already knew many of the people and was greeted with enthusiasm. In fact, he was monopolized from the moment they sat down. Although he smiled warmly at Misty from time to time, she was no longer a priority.

Sophia tried to include her in the conversation, but Misty didn't know any of the people they were talking about, nor had she been to any of the places they discussed. They might as well have been speaking a foreign language. Finally she settled for trying to look interested, which she wasn't. The magic had gone out of the evening.

After a while someone suggested going on to another nightclub. Before Misty could excuse herself, Sophia declined for both of them.

"Misty and I had a long flight, and we're exhausted," she declared, although she didn't look it. "We're going to bed."

"It's only midnight," someone objected. "The evening's just getting started."

There were other objections, but Sophia stood firm. In the general confusion of leave-taking, everyone talked at once, making fragmented plans for the next day. Misty wasn't sure if Brandon even saw her leave. His attention was being claimed by a beautiful redhead.

When they were back in the suite Sophia said, "You didn't want to go to the Salsa Club did you?"

"No, but I wish you had. You would have if I hadn't been here."

"Probably, out of force of habit. But you *are* here, and I'm delighted. I want to spend time with you, pet."

Misty's eyes were troubled. "I don't want to be a millstone around your neck. I didn't really fit in tonight."

"That's absurd! Everyone loved you."

"Oh, sure! If you asked them my name, they'd say Sophia's niece."

Sophia smiled mischievously. "If you asked Brandon mine, he'd say Misty's aunt."

"You made a bigger impression on him than I did." Misty's mouth drooped unconsciously as she told herself it was probably the truth.

"You mean that dreamy expression on his face while he was dancing with you meant he was actually thinking of me?"

Misty rose from the couch restlessly. "He adopts that dreamy expression automatically. Brandon Powers is about as sincere as a used-car salesman!"

"Wouldn't he be marvelous at it?" Sophia remarked admiringly.

"Not if it involved work," Misty snapped. "He's nothing but a useless playboy."

"I wonder." Sophia grew thoughtful. "Something about him doesn't quite ring true."

"What do you mean?"

"I don't exactly know," she said slowly. "His clothes are excellent, he's knowledgeable about food and wine, he knows all the right people."

"I rest my case," Misty replied ironically.

"There's something else, though—a suppressed energy. He's like a racehorse waiting for the gate to go up. The mark of a true playboy is boredom."

Although Misty recalled feeling the same way, she shrugged it off. "Maybe he's new at the game."

"I wonder if he isn't playing one. Suppose that story about being banished from Daddy's bank is just a smoke screen."

"For what?"

"He could be a fortune hunter," Sophia mused.

Misty was reminded of the way Brandon had appraised her expensive outfit, and his remarks about Sophia's necklace. "He did ask if you kept your jewelry in the hotel safe."

Sophia looked amused. "Well, at least we know he's not a jewel thief. Any thief with experience would know these are paste." She touched the glittering stones.

"They look awfully real," Misty said doubtfully.

"I'm glad to hear it. Anyway, what difference does it make? He's perfectly charming. Just use a little bit of caution, darling. But of course that goes for all men."

"If he's a fortune hunter, I'd scarcely be a target. Besides, I won't see him again, except in passing. He didn't even bother to say good-night."

"That wasn't really his fault. Jacqueline was trying to stake a claim. You'll see him again," Sophia said confidently.

Misty continued to think about Brandon as she got ready for bed. Was there really more to him than met the eye? A fortune hunter would be even more repugnant than a playboy. Not that it mattered. Brandon had been merely honing his technique with her until the A Team showed up.

Misty rose early the next morning out of habit. She bathed and dressed quickly, eager for an in-depth look at Rome. The glimpses she'd gotten from the taxi window on the ride from the airport had been fascinating. Venerable churches and narrow, twisting streets gave the city such charm and character. She couldn't wait to explore on her own. Sophia had promised to show her Rome, but Misty wanted to see more than restaurants and night-clubs.

Her aunt's bedroom door was still closed when she was ready to leave, so Misty left a note on the coffee table.

After a continental breakfast in the hotel coffee shop, she went to the concierge's desk in the lobby. He was the man to see for everything from theater tickets to airline reservations. Misty wanted to find out about a sight-seeing tour.

An elderly couple was ahead of her, trying to arrange for a car and driver to take them to a small fishing village nearby. They were also asking about other tourist attractions. It was a lengthy conference.

Misty was patiently waiting her turn when a man joined the line. A casual glance told her he was tall, blond and nice looking.

After fidgeting for a few moments he murmured, "This might take all day."

"I hope not," Misty answered. "I have a lot of historic places to see, and I don't want to spend the first day of my vacation in a hotel lobby."

The man looked faintly surprised. "You're going sightseeing? Haven't you been to Rome before?"

"It was on my list of things to do, but I never got around to it," she answered ironically. Misty was amused at his incredulity. This must be one of Brandon's kind.

He reddened slightly. "Forgive me if I sounded patronizing. I saw you check in last night with a mountain of French luggage, and I just assumed you'd been everywhere."

"That was my aunt's, and she has."

"You're traveling together?"

Before Misty could answer, they were joined by Brandon, looking even more attractive than the night before. He was wearing a navy cashmere sport jacket with fawn-colored slacks. The ascot tucked inside the open neck of his silk shirt made him appear very continental. He could easily have been mistaken for an Italian—one of the fabled lover types.

"What are you doing up this early?" Misty asked. Heaven only knew what time he'd gone to bed.

"I'm an early riser," he answered.

"You must believe in burning the candle at both ends," she remarked.

"If necessary. I don't want to miss anything life has to offer."

"Except work, that is." The blond man smiled to take the sting out of the comment as he joined their conversation. "You probably don't remember me, but we met in London at the Greshams'. My name is Clark Foster."

Brandon's eyes narrowed. "I thought you looked familiar. Was it at the housewarming party they gave at their country estate?"

"Yes, I was the interior designer."

"You did an excellent job," Brandon remarked politely. He turned to Misty. "You two know each other?"

"We haven't met formally," Clark said.

"Are you on vacation also?" she asked after Brandon had introduced them.

Clark shook his head ruefully. "No, I'm a working stiff. I'm here to do a job at the Dedini villa. They're throwing a big party, and I'm transforming the ballroom into a replica of the Garden of Eden."

"With apples on all the trees?" Brandon asked.

"Maybe that's how they plan to tell the guests it's time to leave," Misty observed. "When the witching hour arrives they'll hand everyone an apple and usher them out of paradise. Was the Garden of Eden theme your idea?" she asked Clark.

"No, I just do what I'm told."

"Your work sounds fascinating," Misty said. "You get to decorate fabulous homes all over the world and go to parties in them, besides."

"Yes, I'm fortunate." His smile held a trace of derision. "I'm considered a cut above the other hired help."

The elderly couple at the desk had finally completed their business. As they walked away Misty said, "Will you excuse me? I want to find out about a sight-seeing tour."

"That's no way to see Rome," Brandon said. "I'll take you around."

"No thanks," she answered firmly. "I want to go to all the historic spots."

"Like the Colosseum and the Forum?"

"Exactly."

"That's what I had in mind." He took her hand. "See you around, Clark."

Before Misty could protest, Brandon led her outside and told the doorman to bring his car.

The silver Maserati was exactly the kind of car she would have expected him to drive. It looked powerful and expensive. The interior was the height of luxury, from the glove-leather seats to the thickly carpeted floor and walnut paneling.

"Do you know what all those gadgets are for?" she asked, indicating the bewildering array of dials and knobs on the dashboard.

He grinned. "They're unimportant. The only necessities are good brakes and a horn."

Misty thought he was joking until they merged with the traffic swirling past the hotel. Suddenly they were in a race as accident-prone as the Indy 500. Vans, trucks and cars rushed by them, cutting in and out while the drivers leaned on their horns.

"I see what you mean," she gasped.

"Look out the window," he advised as she gripped the armrest so tightly her knuckles turned white. "This is the famous Via Veneto, and soon we'll be turning onto the Via Condotti. Both are noted for their first-rate shops. You'll be coming here with your aunt, no doubt."

Misty tried to concentrate on the beautifully displayed merchandise and the elegantly clothed people. Everyone was dressed in the height of fashion. The contrast between the modern shops and the ancient, winding streets was fascinating.

A short time later Brandon turned onto a broad avenue that curved past a huge white building festooned with curlicues of marble and classic statuary.

"What is that beautiful building?" Misty exclaimed.

"The Victor Emanuel monument. Some people say it looks like a giant wedding cake. The view from the top is terrific, if you feel like climbing a lot of stairs."

When she nodded eagerly, Brandon parked the car. They climbed dozens of steps to a broad veranda. Another flight of stairs led to a narrow landing. Finally at the very top was the view he'd promised.

All of Rome was spread out below, a fascinating mixture of the old and the new. Churches, stores and apartment houses predominated, but in the midst were partially restored ruins, linking the past to the present.

Misty's eyes were dazzled as she tried to take in everything at once. She pointed out various landmarks and asked Brandon what they were.

He leaned on the parapet and pointed to a stately structure of marble. "That's the Arch of Constantine, and the smaller one in the distance is the Arch of Titus. The round building over there with the openings all around it is the Colosseum."

"Where the Christians were thrown to the lions?"

"Yes, but it was used for many other events, too, like gladiator contests and chariot races. The ancient Romans were very big on sports. The grand opening of the Colosseum was celebrated with daily games for three months. The stadium was built to hold fifty thousand people. Not bad for the year 75 A.D., is it?"

"Were wild animal fights considered games?"

"They were in those days."

Misty shivered slightly. "That's barbaric!"

"A lot of the things they did are unacceptable today, but the Romans were by no means barbarians. Their standard of living was remarkably modern. The upper classes had central heating and running water, also efficient sanitation. When we go to the Forum later you'll see tiled baths and butlers' pantries where the servants kept food warm between courses."

She looked at him admiringly. "You've very knowledgeable about Roman history."

"I've always found it a fascinating subject. It's easy to feel superior about our twentieth-century technology until you realize the debt we owe to people who lived two thousand years ago. Both our language and our law are based on theirs."

"Would you like to have lived in those days?"

His green eyes sparkled with laughter. "Only if I could have been one of the nobles. Slavery isn't for me. I'm allergic to work, remember?"

Misty felt a sudden letdown. Brandon's face had been so animated while he was telling her about an ancient civilization that was both lusty and cultured. She'd forgotten for a moment that he represented the decadence of Rome, not its vigor.

"Your father probably would have been one of the Caesars," she observed dryly.

"And you'd have been a beautiful maiden who lived next door." He reached out to brush away a wind-tossed lock of hair that had curled around her throat.

Misty's skin tingled where his long fingers touched her. "No, with my luck, I'd have been one of the slaves."

"I'd say you've been remarkably blessed."

She tried to ignore the awareness that pulsed between them as his eyes wandered over her features. "I certainly shouldn't complain," she answered matter-of-factly. "This trip to Europe is a dream come true."

"I gather your aunt has lived here for years. Didn't you ever visit her before?"

"She asked me to, but I could never get enough time off work."

"How long do you have now?"

Misty smiled wryly. "I just quit my job. I'm on a permanent vacation."

"We're in the same boat, then."

"Except that you have an income."

"You never know. Maybe you'll meet a dashing duke and get married."

"I'm not looking for a husband."

"You wouldn't have to look far." He stared with frank admiration at her creamy skin and violet eyes. "I'm surprised you're still available—or are you? Is there someone at home waiting for you to have your fling?"

She shook her head. "How about you?"

It was a question she'd been dying to ask. Brandon Powers would be a stunning catch, with or without money. There weren't many men with his charm, good looks, poise and experience. He was obviously not at a loss for female companionship, but was there someone special?

"I'm free as a bird," he assured her.

Misty's heart lifted, even though she knew Brandon wasn't the sort of man one took seriously. If he ever did settle down, it would be with some glittering jet-setter—

and then only temporarily. But he'd added excitement to her first night and day in Rome, and he could make the rest of her stay extremely pleasurable. Providing they kept everything on this light plane.

"Maybe it's a sign," he said in a throaty voice.

"What is?"

"The fact that we met in one of the world's most romantic cities at a time when we're both emotionally unattached."

She refused to be taken in by his practiced charm. "Sophia warned me to be wary of the men here. She said Rome is full of playboys, fortune hunters and jewel thieves."

An inscrutable look hardened Brandon's features. They relaxed instantly into an amused expression. "What category do I fall into?"

"That's pretty obvious. I don't have any money or jewelry."

"You don't need any. There are a lot of things more precious than jewels."

He rubbed his knuckles gently over her cheek. It was an essentially innocent gesture, but Misty felt her heartbeat quicken. The banked fire in his emerald eyes added to her tension. She moistened her lips nervously, then regretted the act when it drew his attention to her mouth.

"Is your skin this soft all over?" he murmured.

"I suppose it's like anyone else's." She managed an offhand tone.

"You're wrong there."

"I'm sure you've made an extensive study of the subject, but I'm more interested in your knowledge of Rome. Where are we going next?"

Brandon chuckled and dropped his hand, not at all abashed by her coolness. "Since you don't care for Roman traffic, I thought we'd take a walk. Would you like to see the Trevi fountain?"

"I'd love to!"

The sexual tension that had sprung up between them was diffused as they strolled down the Via del Corso. The sun shone in a bright blue sky, and a feeling of happiness welled up inside Misty. She was actually in Italy, walking down a Roman street with the most vital man she'd ever met!

As she turned to look at him, he gave her a melting smile and took her hand. An old man walking by patted Brandon on the shoulder and said something in Italian.

Brandon's smile widened into a grin as he answered, *"Grazie."*

"What did you thank him for?" Misty asked.

"He said, 'Good luck, young lovers.'"

She withdrew her hand. "The Italians think every couple are lovers."

"Maybe he's clairvoyant," Brandon teased.

"Or nearsighted," she snapped.

Suppressed laughter tugged at the corners of his firm mouth. "That's the only flaw I can find in you anywhere."

"What is?"

"You're too inhibited."

"Which ought to be a refreshing change," she replied tartly. "That redhead last night certainly didn't suffer from shyness!"

"Jacqueline? She's a woman who knows what she wants."

The reminiscent smile on his face made Misty want to slap him. "My feet are getting tired," she said abruptly. "How much farther is it to the Trevi fountain?"

"Not far, but why don't we stop and have lunch?"

Misty agreed stiffly. She was very put out with Brandon after being reminded of how he'd dropped her the night before, but once he mentioned food she was ravenously hungry. Her breakfast had been very meager and long past.

The little trattoria wasn't elegant, but it had atmosphere. Small round tables covered with checkered cloths each boasted a bottle of Chianti in a straw basket. Waiters in white aprons chatted with the customers like friends, advising them on selections. The whole place was permeated by a delicious aroma coming from the open kitchen, which had garlands of garlic and fat salamis hanging from the low ceiling.

Misty forgot her pique and sighed ecstatically at her first bite of the fettuccine they'd ordered. The broad noodles were coated with a rich sauce of butter, cream and freshly grated parmesan cheese seasoned to perfection.

"I've always loved Italian food, but I've never had anything like this," she said. "I'd gain a hundred pounds if I lived here."

"Scarcely." He looked appreciatively at her slender shoulders and small rounded breasts. "I don't imagine you've ever had a weight problem."

"Not until now." She laughed. "Just wait a few days."

"You were born beautiful. Nothing can change that."

Misty's gaze was troubled as he slipped easily into seductive flattery. "You don't have to put on your usual act for me."

He raised a dark eyebrow. "What would that be?"

"The women you're accustomed to enjoy those soulful looks and insincere compliments, but they just make me uncomfortable."

"What makes you think I'm being insincere?"

"Oh, please, Brandon! You say those things because they're expected."

"Don't tell me you've never had a man tell you you're beautiful, because nobody would buy that."

"Never like you do," she faltered.

"How am I different? You must have heard the same thing from hundreds of men."

Misty's long lashes fluttered down as she reviewed the men she'd known. They were a pretty inept lot next to Brandon. Either they'd come on too strong, putting her off totally, or they'd been so tentative in their passes that she'd felt almost sorry for them. Polished men with exquisite manners had existed for her only in romantic novels.

She was instinctively wary, knowing Brandon could easily sweep her off her feet. Misty was neither a prude nor a starry-eyed idealist. She had subconsciously hoped this trip would include a romantic adventure. But not with someone like Brandon, who wouldn't remember her name next week. The feeling had to be mutual—not merely sexual.

He was regarding her intently. "This goes deeper than a compliment you consider insincere. Every time I've gotten the slightest bit personal, you've withdrawn into your shell. A woman as lovely as you must be accustomed to men trying to know you better. What is it? Did you have a bad experience?"

Nervous laughter welled up in her throat. Brandon would be appalled if he knew how little experience of any kind she had. He would either run for the hills or turn it to his advantage.

He looked tenderly at the fan of dark lashes contrasted against her ivory skin. Placing his hand over hers he said, "I'm sorry, honey. Men can be brutes sometimes, but you don't have to worry about me. I promise I'll never hurt you."

His misunderstanding provided a solution of sorts. If Brandon thought she was suffering from an unhappy love affair, he wouldn't pressure her. Misty didn't want to test her powers of resistance.

She smiled tentatively. "I'd really like to be friends."

The pressure of his fingers increased. "That goes without saying."

"I just thought it was better to have things open and aboveboard between us so you wouldn't feel obligated to give me the full treatment."

"You don't have a very high opinion of me, do you?"

"I'm not being judgmental," she hastened to assure him. "Relationships are very casual in your world. I couldn't live that way."

"I'm glad to hear it." His thumb made slow circles on the soft skin of her wrist. "Maybe our friendship will ripen into something more, and maybe it won't. I'd like to make love to you." His glance at her mouth was almost a physical touch. "I'd like to hold you in my arms and feel your beautiful body catch fire as I discovered all the things that please you."

Misty felt a creeping warmth in her midsection as his low, hypnotic voice evoked sensual images. She could almost feel his long fingers on her receptive body, stroking, exploring, bringing mounting pleasure.

As common sense set in and she tried to jerk away, his hand closed around her wrist. "I'm being honest with you, Misty. That's what I'd *like* to do. I hope you'll feel the same way in time, but either way we'll be friends. Is it a deal?"

She nodded wordlessly.

"Good. Then let's have dessert and decide where we're going from here."

While they finished lunch with whole pears poached in red wine, Misty selected the places she wanted to see.

They went first to the Trevi fountain, where she admired the baroque statue of Neptune being drawn by plunging white horses through jets of dancing water. She dutifully threw a coin over her shoulder, even though Brandon told her the belief that it would ensure a return visit was only a legend originated by a Hollywood movie.

"Don't be cynical," she chided. "Anything can happen if you believe hard enough."

Something stirred in his eyes as he gazed at her animated face. "Okay, you've just made a convert."

They spent hours in the Colosseum and after that the Forum, wandering among the ruins with a sense of wonder. The same columns and arches had stood there when Julius Caesar was alive. Cicero might have walked on the rocky path they strolled along, and later, maybe Michelangelo.

When shadows began to darken the archways, and the pillars in the distance became indistinct, they started toward the exit—reluctantly on Misty's part.

"I have a feeling the senators are about to arrive in their chariots at any minute," she said as Brandon hailed a cab to take them back to his car. "I wish we could stay and see them in their togas and laurel wreaths."

He put his arm around her. "You have to live in the present, not the past."

As Misty looked up into his strong face, she was inclined to agree with him.

She had been nervous when Brandon drove, but Misty was a basket case in the taxi. The driver handled the car like a kamikaze pilot. She turned pale when a truck and a van converged on them from either side, both bent on occupying their space. The cabdriver took it as a personal offense. He let go of the wheel to shake his fist and lean on the horn while muttering words that didn't require a knowledge of Italian to be understood.

"Don't watch the road," Brandon advised, trying to contain his amusement.

"*Somebody* should!" she gasped.

"Think about something else."

"Like what? Whether my life insurance is paid up?"

"I have a better idea."

He took her in his arms and cradled her body close. As she stiffened in protest his mouth covered hers. His lips were gentle yet persuasive, inviting participation rather than demanding it.

Misty felt herself responding automatically. His subtle male scent was like an aphrodisiac, coupled with the close embrace that acquainted her with the tensile strength of his lean body.

When he felt her relax, Brandon made a tiny sound of satisfaction. His fingers wound through her silky hair, holding her while his warm mouth trailed over her cheek, although Misty couldn't have moved away.

She felt disoriented when the taxi stopped.

Brandon smiled into her dazzled eyes. "Did that help?"

"Help?" she asked vaguely.

"You forgot about the traffic."

"Oh . . . oh, yes." Her fair skin flushed as she realized how easily he had accomplished his purpose. She struggled to match his poise. "Thanks. I couldn't have done it without you."

He grinned. "Glad to be of assistance. In the future we'll have to take a lot more taxis."

Brandon was so completely natural that Misty forgot her embarrassment. By the time they arrived at the hotel they were back on a friendly, joking basis.

The only thing that bothered her slightly was the fact that he didn't ask for any future dates. But Misty reminded herself that Brandon knew many people in Rome. He'd probably made a lot of plans before he met her.

Sophia was talking on the phone when Misty let herself into the suite. She hung up promptly and said, "Where on earth have you been all day?"

"Sight-seeing. Didn't you get my note?"

"Yes, but I expected you back before this. Where did you go?"

"Everywhere! We spent hours at the Colosseum, and then—"

"We?" Sophia homed in on the part that interested her.

"I, uh, I met Brandon Powers in the lobby when I went down to take a bus tour. He offered to drive me instead."

"I knew you'd made a conquest!"

"Our meeting was just a lucky coincidence," Misty protested.

"Naturally. He had nothing better to do than spend a whole day poking around old ruins."

"They're very interesting," Misty said defensively.

"No doubt. But I don't think that's what Brandon was interested in."

"You're making a big deal out of nothing." Since that could very well be true, she didn't want her aunt to expect a romance to blossom.

"All right, but you're not being any fun. At least tell me where else he's taking you."

"I don't have any plans to see him again." Misty tried very hard to sound bored by the whole subject.

"I see." Sophia slanted a glance at her niece's mobile face. "Well, I'm glad you didn't make plans for tonight, because I made a date for us."

"You didn't have to include me. I'll be perfectly all right on my own."

"Don't be ridiculous, darling."

"No, really, Sophia. I want you to do exactly what you would if I weren't here."

"I am. We have a dinner date with a charming young man."

"And you always go out as a threesome," Misty remarked dryly.

"Actually, you're the one he really wants to take out. I'm just getting a free ride."

"You expect me to believe that?"

"Well, he used your name to strike up an acquaintance."

"You haven't been picking up men again!"

"Relax, pet. This one picked *me* up."

"What am I going to do with you?" Misty groaned. "Brandon turned out to be harmless, but what do you know about this new one?"

"I wouldn't call Brandon Powers harmless. I have this funny feeling about him. There is something he's not telling," Sophia remarked thoughtfully. "Did you find out any more about him today?"

"What is there to find out? He told us who he is and where he came from."

"And you believed him?"

"Why shouldn't I?"

"Why indeed?" Sophia murmured.

"If you think he's a phony, why are you urging me to see more of him?"

"I'm not advocating marriage—just a charming little interlude. Besides, Brandon is the most fascinating male on the continent. It would be utterly delicious if you were to snatch him away from all those man-eaters who are after him."

"He's way out of my league." Misty gave up the pretense that she wasn't interested.

"That's negative thinking," Sophia scolded.

"No, I'm just being realistic."

"Didn't he give you *any* encouragement?"

Misty hesitated, remembering the kiss in the taxi. But that had been a joke on Brandon's part. He wasn't affected by it as she'd been.

"Not really." She sighed.

"What did you talk about all day?" Sophia persisted.

"Ancient history mostly."

"I can't believe a man like Brandon Powers spent a whole day discussing the rise and fall of the Roman empire, not with a beautiful girl. He has Romeo written all over his gorgeous face. You can't be telling me the whole story."

Misty thought about Brandon's declaration that he'd like to make love to her. That was the sort of detail Sophia wanted, but she wasn't about to give it to her.

"Sorry to disappoint you," she said lightly. "Obviously I'm not his Juliet. If you're looking for romance you'll have to find it yourself."

"I must admit I *am* disappointed. You two made such a stunning couple, but Clark isn't bad, either." Sophia wasn't one to dwell on failure.

"Who's Clark?" Misty asked warily.

"He said you'd met this morning."

"Not that I recall." Misty had completely forgotten the other man after a day with Brandon.

"Clark Foster. Tall, blond, little mustache." Sophia jogged her memory.

"Oh, the interior decorator. Yes, we met in the lobby. I can't say I was too impressed, though. He seemed like a terrible snob."

"You mustn't jump to conclusions so quickly," Sophia chided. "I thought he was quite charming."

"Then you go out with him."

"Don't be difficult," her aunt said impatiently. "It should be a very instructive evening. Clark has done some of the most famous homes on the continent. I've been in many of them. The man really knows his craft."

"It does sound like an interesting job," Misty admitted. "I guess I was just put off by something he said. But you're right, I shouldn't be so judgmental."

Sophia nodded. "Meeting someone new is like encountering an iceberg. The part you see doesn't give you any idea of what's hidden under the surface. Clark Foster might turn out to be quite a surprise."

"Isn't that what you felt about Brandon?"

"He's already been a surprise." Sophia's slight frown smoothed. "But I still say we haven't seen the last of that divine man."

Misty stood up. "You can sit here and think about him. I'm going to take a shower."

Chapter Three

Misty and her aunt met Clark in the hotel cocktail lounge by prearrangement. As he stood politely to greet them, Misty took a closer look than she had that morning.

Clark didn't have Brandon's eye-catching looks or instant magnetism, but he made a nice appearance. In a dark, well-cut suit he was very presentable.

"Have we kept you waiting?" Sophia asked.

"No, you're right on time." Clark summoned a waiter. "What can I get you to drink?" After they'd ordered, he said to Misty, "I'm so glad you could make it on such short notice."

"I'm not the one with all the dates. Sophia is the popular member of the family."

"I'm honored to be dining with both of you," Clark replied.

"I told you he was charming." Sophia nodded approvingly.

"My aunt tells me you're also quite talented," Misty said.

"You're familiar with my work?" he asked Sophia.

"I was a guest at the Grenvilles' château right after you finished it," she answered.

"I thought it came out quite well, although the pink brocade in the drawing room wouldn't have been my choice," he said wryly.

"Don't you get to do what you want?" Misty asked. "After all, they're paying for your expertise."

"That would seem to make sense, but when you're dealing with the moneyed classes you learn to subordinate your own tastes."

"I don't think money enters into it," Sophia said. "No matter how knowledgeable you are at decorating, people have to live with the results after you go on to greener pastures."

"That's correct. But pink brocade?" He raised his eyes to the ceiling. "I had to force myself to order the fabric."

"All of life is a compromise," Sophia remarked mildly. "Few of us get to do exactly as we'd like, unfortunately."

"Very true, dear lady. Besides, I'm well paid for my efforts."

"Still, I can understand what you're saying," Misty said. "It can't be very satisfying to do something that goes against your own instincts."

A little smile lifted the corners of his rather thin lips. "Satisfaction comes in many ways."

"I suppose you're quite a celebrity at the parties afterward."

"Hardly. I'm more like a chef who's called in for a pat on the back after an excellent meal."

"You're too modest," Sophia said.

"I prefer to let my work speak for me."

"What marvelous things are you doing to the Dedini villa?" she asked. "I didn't know it needed refurbishing."

"I'm only working on the ballroom. This is rather a departure for me. I've never done a theme party before."

"You certainly have your work cut out for you," Sophia commented. "Last year's will be hard to top."

"Do they have one of these things every year?" Misty asked.

Sophia nodded. "To celebrate their anniversary. It's become a tradition. The Count also gives his wife, Elise, something smashing as a gift. He presents it at midnight with appropriate fanfare."

"Isn't that a little ostentatious?" Misty asked.

"I guess he figures if you've got it, flaunt it," Clark remarked.

"Last year he gave her pearls so big the oysters must have been taking vitamins," Sophia said. "And the year before it was a floor-length sable cape."

"What can he possibly do for an encore?" Misty asked.

"I understand he had his agent bidding at the recent auction of that late drugstore heiress's jewel collection. The rumor is that Count Dedini was high bidder for the diamond necklace with the Star of Venus in the pendant," Sophia said.

"And she's going to wear it at a party with hundreds of people?" Misty gasped. "I hope it's insured."

"Don't worry, the place will be crawling with security men," Clark said.

"Besides, it's a private party for their friends," Sophia said.

"You got *me* an invitation, and I've never met them," Misty pointed out.

"Are you planning to make off with the loot?" Clark joked.

"No, I'm just saying everyone there won't necessarily be a friend."

"I'm sure they've taken every precaution," Sophia answered. "Count Dedini might be a trifle ostentatious, as you say, but he isn't a fool."

Clark shrugged. "He can also afford to lose his little bauble if worse came to worst. It wouldn't be a tragedy."

"Speaking of baubles," Sophia remarked.

She was looking over Clark's shoulder at a stunning blonde who had her hand on Brandon's shoulder. A huge diamond glittered on her finger as she slowly caressed the soft fabric of his jacket. He was looking down at her with a tolerant smile.

"Isn't that Bootsy Oberfein with Brandon Powers?" Sophia asked. "Her father is the grocery-chain magnate," she told Misty.

"Money attracts money," Clark observed acidly.

"I don't think he's counting her assets," Misty commented with equal tartness.

"Not her frozen ones anyway." Clark's laugh had a slightly lewd sound. "But why should he, when he has a whole bank to draw on?"

"You know Brandon?" Sophia asked.

"I've run across him a few times, but he never remembers me."

"He owns a bank, you say?" Sophia inquired casually.

"His family does. Powers is the black sheep." Clark snickered. "I hear they pay him to stay away. It should happen to me."

"You wouldn't want to give up the work you do so divinely and enjoy so much," Sophia said blandly.

Misty gazed sharply at her aunt. Sophia was being a little too ingenuous. Had she become disenchanted with Clark for some reason? And why was she checking up on Brandon? Did she really have serious doubts about him?

"I guess you're right." Clark expanded under Sophia's flattery. "But it just burns me to see the way some people waltz through life without ever having to pay their dues."

"I suppose that includes me," Sophia remarked.

He looked chagrined. "Not at all, dear lady. I hope you don't think I was speaking personally."

"I'm not exactly useful," she answered mildly.

"That's not true, and you know it!" Misty exclaimed. "My aunt is on the board of several philanthropic organizations," she told Clark.

"I'm sure you do wonderful work." He concentrated earnestly on Sophia, anxious to make up for any imagined slight.

"I wouldn't call it work, but it's satisfying to try to alleviate a little of the misery of the world."

"That was exactly my point. You come from the same background of unlimited means." Clark was too intent to see Sophia's slight smile. "Yet you choose to do something useful with your life rather than merely enjoying yourself twenty-four hours a day."

"Do you really feel that's an achievable goal? I might almost be tempted to give up my committees if I thought so."

Clark was adept at sensing when he'd overstepped an invisible boundary. He sat back in his chair, smiling ruefully. "You must excuse me for climbing up on a soapbox. I enjoy playing the devil's advocate when I find someone so intellectually stimulating."

"Then you don't really hate rich people?"

"Definitely not! I might even be one of them someday." He signaled the waiter. "Shall we have another drink? Our dinner reservations aren't for another half hour."

Sophia shivered slightly. "While you're ordering I think I'll go up to the suite and get my stole. There seems to be a draft in here. Do you feel it, Misty?"

"No, but I'm dressed more warmly than you."

Misty was wearing a pale blue silk dress with a matching jacket, while Sophia's wine-colored gown had a wide neckline that just skimmed her shoulders. It was a perfect showcase for the magnificent necklace of cabochon rubies around her throat.

"Let me get your wrap for you," Clark offered.

"That would be lovely." Sophia opened her evening bag and brought out her key. "It's lying on a chair in my bedroom. I meant to bring it with me, but I forgot."

"No problem. I'll be right back."

"Are you out of your mind?" Misty erupted after Clark had left. "How could you give him your key?"

"He'd have difficulty getting in without it."

"This is no laughing matter! What do you know about Clark Foster?"

"He's no mental genius, but I'm sure he can find his way up in an elevator and down again."

"You know what I mean, Sophia! He could be a thief for all you know."

Sophia laughed. "He'd be in for a disappointment in *our* suite. Besides, Clark isn't that stupid. He'd be the prime suspect if anything was missing when we returned."

"Tonight maybe, but suppose he made an impression of the key?"

"You've been watching too much television."

"And you're too trusting," Misty scolded. "I'm supposed to be the naïve one, and you hand your key to a perfect stranger!"

"Scarcely perfect. I hate to admit it, pet, but you were right. The man is a crashing bore."

"Because he criticized your friends?"

"No, I criticize them myself on occasion. It's Clark's whining I object to."

"He did seem fairly disapproving of their life-styles."

"I can't abide a hypocrite. He'd change places in one minute flat. All that hoopla about the work ethic! If any of those idle rich he's complaining about were to take a job, Clark would be the first one to howl that they were snatching bread out of the mouths of the poor."

Misty grinned. "Maybe now you won't be so fast to pick up strange men."

"They never turned out to be *that* strange," Sophia complained. Her eyes brightened as she noticed the tall dark man making his way toward them. "Besides, you have to admit Brandon turned out to be a gem."

Brandon arrived at their table before Misty could answer. "I hope you didn't mind my kidnapping your niece for the whole day," he said to Sophia.

"No, it was very kind of you to take her sight-seeing. She told me what a fabulous time she had."

Misty could cheerfully have strangled her aunt. How could she give Brandon the impression that the day had been special for her? Even though it had.

"I'm glad," he answered warmly. "It was memorable for me, too."

"We were so fortunate to meet you," Sophia remarked innocently. "I have a million appointments over the next few days, and I would have felt badly about leaving Misty on her own, since she doesn't know her way around Rome."

Misty made a strangled sound. Sophia's behavior was outrageous, even for her! "You don't have to worry about me," she said stiffly. "I'm past the age when I need a nursemaid."

"But just the right age for an escort." Brandon's eyes sparkled with merriment. "Can I apply for the job?"

"No, you cannot! You know perfectly well what Sophia is doing. She did the same thing to you last night. Why do you let yourself be manipulated?"

"I'm not being," he answered gently before giving Sophia an amused look. "Your aunt merely anticipated my moves before I could make them."

"That's a polite way of saying she orchestrated them." Misty scowled.

"Not at all. What man wouldn't consider himself lucky to have a date with you?" His husky voice teased her nerve endings.

"I hope you realize how embarrassing this is," she mumbled. "I haven't felt this awkward since I wore braces and Billy Edwards tried to kiss me."

"Their braces locked," Sophia explained.

Brandon lifted Misty's chin in his palm and scrutinized her with mock seriousness. "That's no longer a problem," he said.

She smiled in spite of herself. "How do you know? You can't see my teeth."

"I can now, and they're beautiful—like the rest of you." One long forefinger ran slowly over her bottom teeth.

The joking gesture evoked a shockingly erotic feeling. Misty sat back in her chair. "You're living dangerously," she said coldly. "How do you know I don't bite?"

"I'm willing to take a chance."

"She didn't even misbehave when she was little," Sophia assured Brandon. "Misty was such a well brought up child; it was downright unnatural."

"I thought I was your favorite niece," Misty reminded her.

"You still are, pet. That's why I'm determined to see that you have some fun."

Brandon chuckled. "I gather I've been picked to provide it. Are you suggesting I lead your niece astray?"

"Don't you dare," Sophia warned. "I just want you to teach her to kick up her heels, instill a little joie de vivre in her."

He grinned mischievously. "It won't be as much fun as seducing her, but okay, it's a deal."

"Not with me, it isn't!" Misty was bursting with indignation. "Don't I have anything to say about this?"

"We'll discuss it over dinner tomorrow night," he answered soothingly.

"Absolutely not! Just once I'd like to have a date that wasn't arranged for me."

"You drive a hard bargain, but all right, we'll make it lunch. That's my own idea, not Sophia's." Before Misty could protest further, he squeezed her hand. "See you tomorrow, honey."

Misty was speechless as she watched him walk away with an easy, confident gait. She recovered when she turned back to Sophia.

"I've never been this humiliated in my entire life! Why didn't you just offer him money to take me out?"

"You're overreacting, darling," Sophia replied calmly. "Brandon's too clever to be maneuvered into something he didn't really want to do. If I were you, I'd count my blessings. He's a real prize. I'd be in there competing for him myself if I were ten years younger." She smiled impishly. "Well, maybe fifteen years."

Misty's resentment drained away as she gazed at her aunt's unlined face framed by a halo of bright curls. Sophia was just trying to make this vacation outstanding. Her methods might be reprehensible, but her motives were pure.

"You could compete right now," Misty said sincerely.

"Not against pansy-colored eyes and a figure that was made for a bikini," Sophia responded fondly. "Do you know how much fun you could have if you'd just loosen up and accept what life has to offer?"

Misty could imagine what Brandon had to offer, and the thought made her knees feel weak. Perhaps Sophia was right. Excitement fizzed suddenly in her veins. Maybe she could never match her aunt's ease with people or embrace her reckless philosophy completely, but she was certainly going to try!

Misty's mouth curved upward as she noticed Clark entering the lounge. "Am I having fun yet?"

"The game is young. Just call this a foul ball." Sophia's face didn't betray her emotions as Clark joined them. "There you are. We were wondering what happened to you."

He handed her a wine-colored stole that matched her dress. "A tour group just checked in. The lobby is a madhouse. I had a devil of a time getting on an elevator."

"Well, you're here now, that's what matters. Isn't it, Misty?" Sophia's expression was innocent as she looked at her niece, but her eyes held a sparkle of amusement.

Misty overslept the next morning. The unaccustomed activity and excitement, plus the difference in time zones, caught up with her belatedly.

She jumped out of bed when she awoke and saw how late it was. Brandon hadn't mentioned a time or place for their luncheon date, but she wanted to be ready when he called.

Her haste was justified. Brandon didn't phone; he came to the suite. Misty was zipping her beige wool skirt when she heard a knock at the door. She tucked in her cream-colored silk blouse and buckled an alligator belt around her trim waist, expecting Sophia to answer the door. When the knock was repeated she realized her aunt must have gone out. Stepping hurriedly into a pair of pumps, she ran into the living room.

When she opened the door, Brandon raised an eyebrow at her breathless state. "Am I too early?"

"No, I'm almost ready. You didn't say when you were coming, though. I expected you to call first."

"I can come back later," he offered.

"It's okay. I just have to get my purse."

Brandon was looking thoughtfully around the suite when he heard Misty's small exclamation. He followed her into the bedroom.

"Is anything wrong?" he asked.

She was searching through one of the drawers in a large carved dresser. "I can't find my locket."

His eyes narrowed slightly. "Was it valuable?"

"Only to me. It was my grandmother's."

"You put it in that drawer?"

She nodded. "Under my slips. Not that it's costly enough to steal, but I didn't like to leave it lying around."

"Let me take a look."

Brandon unfolded the lacy garments in the corner of the drawer. After inspecting each one, he deftly folded it again and put it on top of the dresser. Then he started on the stack of panties in the middle.

Misty's face warmed. There was something subtly erotic about having him inspect her lingerie that intimately. "I know I didn't put it there," she said hurriedly.

"We might as well make sure." Next he lifted out her panty hose. "Is this what you're looking for?" He held up a small gold heart on a fine chain.

"You found it!" She uttered a happy cry.

"Now you see why it's wise to be thorough."

Misty frowned slightly. "I could have sworn I put this under my slips. How could I have hidden it under my panty hose? The chain might have snagged them. I must really be losing my grip."

"We all get a little absentminded at times. I only hope Sophia isn't as careless about *her* jewels," he added casually.

"This isn't exactly a jewel, but I would have felt terrible if I'd lost it." She was fumbling with the tiny catch.

"Here, let me do that."

He turned her around. While Misty held her long hair out of the way, Brandon fastened the delicate clasp.

When he was finished he kissed the sensitive nape of her neck.

His warm lips sent a shiver down Misty's spine. She started to move away, but his arms wrapped around her from behind, drawing her against his long length.

"Sweet little Misty." His mouth slid slowly along her jawline. "You're so incredibly lovely."

Her first impulse was to pull away. Brandon was arousing emotions that alarmed her. Then she remembered her resolution of the night before.

Resting her head on his shoulder, she murmured, "Tell me how lovely."

"I'd have to be a poet." He turned her in his arms and gazed down at her with glowing eyes.

She put her arms around his neck, tilting her face up. "Then show me," she whispered.

His lips touched hers gently, savoring the sensory pleasure. Misty closed her eyes to enjoy the inexpressible feeling. Her body relaxed and flowed against his like honey warmed by a low flame.

Brandon's arms tightened at her receptiveness. His hands stroked her back, molding her against him until they were joined from shoulder to thigh. Until she was quiveringly aware of every hard masculine plane of his body, every taut muscle.

When his tongue delicately traced the outline of her closed lips, they opened like a flower to a hummingbird. His tongue probed sensuously, suggestively, arousing an almost primitive response. She wound her arms more tightly around his neck.

Brandon's small groan of satisfaction vibrated in his throat while his tongue plunged deeply with male expertise. Misty clung to him as his tongue advanced and retreated, lighting tiny fires inside her. Before they could burn out of control, the chambermaid appeared in the doorway.

"*Scusi.*" The woman backed away hurriedly. "I come back later."

Misty jerked away from Brandon, her cheeks flaming.

"My suite is already made up," he murmured.

She hesitated. Was that what she really wanted? On a purely sexual basis the answer was clear. Brandon could bring the kind of pleasure she'd only dreamed about. Her body was still vibrating from the small sample he'd bestowed. But shouldn't there be more than physical gratification?

He watched the chaotic thoughts flash across her expressive face. "Why don't we take a walk before lunch?" he suggested gently.

"Yes, I... That would be nice." She avoided looking at him.

He cupped her chin in his hand and tilted her face up. "Look at me, Misty." When she complied reluctantly he said, "Don't worry about it, honey. I think we're destined to make love, but not until you're ready. When the time comes, I'll be waiting."

She swallowed painfully. "You must think I'm some kind of freak."

"Not necessarily." His green eyes lit with laughter. "Don't you think I've ever been turned down before?"

"Not often, I'll bet. You're very... persuasive."

He chuckled. "Evidently not persuasive enough. Well, if you want to waste your time looking at the grandeurs of Rome instead of spending the day in my arms, that's your decision." He put his arm around her shoulders and led her to the door.

Misty appreciated the way Brandon always dispelled her embarrassment. But as he nestled her body against his, she couldn't help regretting her decision.

When they were outside on the sidewalk he asked, "Anyplace special you'd like to go?"

"No, I just want to look in the shop windows."

Brandon consulted the thin gold watch on his wrist. "We'll have to make tracks. The stores close at one and don't open again until four."

"They certainly keep funny hours here," Misty remarked as they started down a narrow cobblestone street.

"The custom makes a lot of sense when you think about it, though. American men only get to see their children for a brief period before bedtime when everyone's tired and cranky. Europeans spend a relaxing couple of hours together in the middle of the day."

"I guess it's sensible when you put it that way, but I'd never get used to having lunch at two and dinner at ten."

"Everything's relative. We grab a hamburger for lunch or thaw something frozen for dinner, which *they* think is strange. Italians dine; Americans eat. There's a big difference."

"I'll have to agree. That pasta yesterday was divine. Could we go back there today?"

"Rome is full of places equally good. Let's be adventurous."

"Whatever you say," she agreed promptly.

He laughed. "I wish you meant that."

"Don't try to sweet-talk me," she answered lightly. "You're just trying to get out of buying me lunch."

"It won't work?"

"No way. I'm starving. I'm going to order everything on the menu."

"How about an aperitif to tide you over?" he suggested.

The narrow street curved unexpectedly into a wide piazza with the inevitable fountain. This one was much less imposing than the Trevi but perhaps more charming in its own way. Laughing children frolicked among dolphins and turtles while jets of water played on their sleek bronze heads.

Several cafés with gaily striped awnings had sidewalk tables outside. They sat down at one of them. Misty hadn't really wanted a drink, but the aperitif Brandon ordered for her didn't have a harsh bite. The amber liquid in the diminutive glass tasted nonalcoholic. It soothed her empty stomach and warmed her blood.

"Mmm, this is delicious." She licked her lips appreciatively. "They're awfully stingy with it though, aren't they?"

"It's a lot more potent than it tastes," he warned.

"A child couldn't get tipsy on this small amount," she scoffed. "I'm sure I could handle another one."

As Brandon beckoned to the waiter, a strolling musician entered the square. He was colorfully dressed, and his voice was melodic. Misty was entranced. The ancient square paved with worn cobblestones was like a stage setting, the splashing fountain providing background music.

"If this were a movie, everyone would get up and dance," she commented.

"Shall we lead the way?" Brandon stood up and held out his arms.

"Why not?" Misty would never have considered such extroverted behavior at home, but it seemed like a perfectly natural thing to do at that moment.

They waltzed around the fountain while everyone watched approvingly and the musician followed, serenading them. Misty was completely carefree, whirling in Brandon's arms. It felt wonderful to do exactly as she pleased for once in her life. Sheer delight filled her.

The people sitting around the piazza applauded when the dance ended. Brandon gave the musician some coins before leading Misty back to their table.

"I can't believe I just did that." She looked at him with a pleased expression.

"Maybe you're finally losing some of your inhibitions."

"You seem to have that effect on me." She tilted her head back and drained her glass.

"I hope so," he murmured.

The potent liqueur loosened her inhibitions further. "Do you really like me as a person, Brandon, or are you just interested in the chase?"

"I really like you," he said solemnly, although his eyes twinkled.

"I'm not as sophisticated as those other women you run around with," she said doubtfully.

"That's a pure plus."

"Be honest." She piled her long glossy hair on top of her head. "Would you like me better with a fancy hairdo and high-style clothes?"

He couldn't contain his amusement any longer. "If you really want me to be honest, I'd like you best with no clothes at all."

"I'm serious, Brandon!"

"So am I. But you've had one too many drinks on an empty stomach. Since I never take advantage of tipsy women, we'd better have lunch."

"I am not drunk," she said with dignity.

"Maybe not, but you're sure relaxed." He grinned.

She slanted him a look from under long eyelashes. "Isn't that the way you want me to be?"

"Not artificially." He drew her to her feet and kissed the tip of her nose. "I want you in full possession of your faculties when I make love to you."

"Don't you mean *if*?"

"I think we both know the answer to that." He took her hand. "Come on, let's get some food into you before you make me a proposition I can't refuse."

"You're no fun at all," she grumbled.

"I'll remind you of that," he promised.

Hand in hand they retraced their steps until they found a small restaurant much like the one from the day before. Brandon was right about the quality of the food in Rome. Their prosciutto and melon, followed by linguine with white clam sauce, was delicious.

"Maybe I'd better not have any wine," Misty said as the effects of her aperitifs started to wear off.

"Are you afraid I might forget my scruples?" he teased.

She smiled wryly. "No, I'm afraid I'll forget mine. I never said exactly what I thought to a man before."

"Why not?"

"Mostly because it wasn't very complimentary. With you it's different."

"I'm flattered," he said.

"I can't decide if you bring out the best or the worst in me."

"How can it be bad to follow your instincts?" he asked deeply.

"That's what Sophia does, but she's made at least one mistake. I don't really know anything about you."

"What would you like to know?"

Misty stared at him with a slight frown. "Sophia thinks you haven't told us everything about yourself, and I can't help agreeing with her."

Brandon returned her gaze steadily. "Obviously I haven't told you my life history. We haven't spent that much time together. You're free to ask any questions, though."

"I don't want to give you the third degree," she mumbled.

"It's quite all right. My life is pretty much an open book. It's hard to keep a secret when everyone knows everyone else and gossip is the major pastime. What was it that aroused your suspicions?" There was a hint of wariness under his relaxed manner.

"I didn't say I was suspicious," Misty protested. "I'd just like to know more about you. Little things," she concluded lamely.

"I'm told I was a beautiful baby."

"You don't have to start *that* far back."

"Well, let's see. How about the time Jimmy Vandercott and I invented the airmail special delivery letter during a game of post office at Amy Waring's birthday party?"

"From there you went on to delivering overnight express mail in college, no doubt," Misty said dryly.

"How did you know?"

"Just a lucky guess. I can see you aren't going to be responsive about your past, so how about the present?"

"It's too nice a day for a lecture. You already know about my present, and you don't approve."

"I never said that," she protested.

"Maybe not in so many words, but you have a very expressive face."

"I'm sorry. I have no right to be critical. A lot of men would like to be in your position—Clark Foster, for one."

"Who?"

"You know, the interior decorator we were talking to yesterday morning. He says you've met several times before."

"Oh, yes." Brandon's eyes narrowed thoughtfully. "He does seem to pop up fairly regularly."

"Clark isn't exactly a member of the jet set, but he apparently gets invited everywhere because of his business connections."

"Entrée into the haut monde isn't difficult." Brandon smiled sardonically. "All you have to be is rich, amusing or useful."

"I think Clark resents being patronized."

"Then he'll just have to work at getting rich."

Misty wasn't really concerned with Clark's problems. Brandon's plans were what interested her. "Do you still intend to be here for the Dedini party?" she asked casually.

"I wouldn't miss it," he assured her.

"Where will you go after that?"

"Who knows? Possibly back to America, if all goes well."

"I see." Misty's feathery lashes veiled her eyes as she inspected her plate with pretended interest.

"We have two weeks until the party." Brandon's big hand covered hers. "Anything can happen in that time."

"True." She smiled gallantly.

Two weeks wasn't much time to form a relationship. But if that's all there was going to be, she'd make the most of it. Maybe it was better this way. She wouldn't have time to do anything foolish—like fall in love.

"I'll know everything there is to know about Rome by then," she remarked brightly.

"I was thinking of something more personal," he murmured.

"You'll have to follow me around the city," she warned. "You know what a demon tourist I am. I can't wait to get started again."

Brandon looked at his watch. "I'm tied up for the rest of the day, honey. I have to meet someone at the airport."

She tried hard to hide her disappointment. "I understand."

"I'm sorry. I didn't expect him until later in the week."

Misty felt better that it was a man instead of a woman. "Is he a friend or a relative?"

"Neither. He's a—" Brandon paused. "I guess you could call him an obligation. I went to college with Jim, but I haven't seen him in years."

"What time do you have to meet him?"

"Soon, but we have time for dessert."

The zabaglione Brandon ordered was delicious, a light confection of eggs, sugar and marsala wine whipped to a rich, smooth cream. Misty would have preferred to linger over it, but she could tell that Brandon was anxious to leave. He seemed a little preoccupied.

After he left her at the hotel Misty went up to the suite, undecided about what she wanted to do for the rest of the afternoon. She felt more than a little let down that Brandon hadn't made another date.

It was understandable that he'd spend this evening with his friend, but how about the next night, or the night after? Surely the man had plans of his own.

Was Brandon purposely keeping her off base, or was he confident that she'd be available whenever he got around to her? Neither explanation was very palatable.

Sophia came out of her bedroom when she heard Misty's key in the lock. "I didn't expect you so early. I thought you and Brandon might spend the day together."

"He had to pick up a friend at the airport."

"Did you have a nice lunch?"

"Yes, the food was fabulous."

Sophia waited for further details. When none were forthcoming she said, "If you don't have plans for tonight, we've been invited to a party. A lot of the younger set will be there. I think you'll enjoy it."

"I don't know." Misty was looking discontentedly at herself in a Venetian mirror over the down-filled sofa. "I don't have anything to wear."

"We have all afternoon to go shopping."

Misty gathered her long, shining hair in both hands. "Do you think I ought to have my hair cut short?"

"Definitely not. It could stand some styling, though. I'll take you to Alexander. He's a genius. But first we'll go shopping."

Misty began to have a pleasurable feeling of excitement. She had to make things clear from the start, however. "I'm going to pay for everything myself, and I can't afford your famous designers."

"Don't worry, couturier clothes take weeks of fittings, but their prêt-à-porter lines are quite decent at a fraction of the cost."

Misty smiled. "That's a pretty fancy name for ready-to-wear."

"What's in a name? You'll be the most stunning girl at the party. The men will race each other to get to you."

"Promise you won't point them in my direction."

"I won't have to."

"Promise me, Sophia!" Misty demanded. "Your two previous tries at fixing me up weren't a howling success."

"I'll admit Clark was a mistake, but Brandon would scarcely be considered a washout."

"He isn't exactly taking up all my time, either," Misty answered grimly.

"That's his loss. Soon he'll have to stand in line to get a date with you."

Misty laughed. "If confidence were cash, you'd be a millionaire."

"Who needs money? We have something better— brains and beauty. Come on, pet, let's go buy out Rome."

Chapter Four

Misty discovered an unexpected streak of extravagance in herself on the shopping tour with her aunt.
Maybe the desired metamorphosis was taking place, and
she was becoming more like Sophia. Strangely enough,
the older woman was the one who urged restraint.

"That isn't a good buy," Sophia said when Misty en-
thused over a shocking-pink evening gown with huge
puffed sleeves and an intricately draped skirt.

"I don't care," Misty answered recklessly. "You said
yourself that money is to spend."

"For people who have plenty of it. Those who don't
have to choose wisely."

"I've done that all my life," Misty protested. "I'm
tired of sensible little silk dresses with jackets, and good
quality skirts and sweaters that will last several seasons."

"That wasn't what I had in mind," her aunt said mildly.

"Good, because for once I intend to be wildly impractical." Misty was holding the dress against her body, looking in the mirror with shining eyes. "I want to look *glamorous*!"

"You will, pet, but not in that dress."

"What's wrong with it? I'll bet everybody would notice me."

"That's the problem. You wouldn't get more than one or two wearings out of it."

"I didn't think *you'd* turn practical on me."

"It's one of the survival skills I learned when I ceased to be rich," Sophia replied dryly. "I substitute ingenuity for extravagance."

"You didn't on *that* outfit."

Misty eyed her aunt's chic black suit. The tailored lines were softened by a frilly pink lace blouse that had a double flounced collar and delicate lace ruffles extending past her jacket cuffs.

"Your suit is stunning. Is it new? I've never seen it before."

"You've seen it dozens of times," Sophia assured her. "Sometimes I wear the skirt with a white jacket, or the jacket with a pleated checked skirt. Other times I wear the complete suit with a black cashmere sweater or a tailored white linen blouse."

Misty had seen her in the outfits she described. "You mean that's the same suit?" she exclaimed.

Sophia nodded. "The possibilities are endless. The trick is to put your money into good basics, then accessorize."

Misty looked longingly at the shocking-pink gown. "That's all right for daytime clothes, but I want something smashing to wear at night."

"Go into the dressing room while I pick out a few things for you to try on."

Sophia appeared a short time later, followed by a saleswoman loaded down with shimmering garments.

"Put these on." She held out a pair of black satin pants. "They'll go with practically anything."

Misty complied, but her eyebrows rose as she looked in the mirror. The tight-fitting pants outlined every curve of her long legs and molded to her bottom like the skin on a peach.

"Don't you think they're a trifle snug? Maybe I'd better have the next size."

"Nonsense! They're absolutely perfect," Sophia decreed.

Misty was looking doubtfully over her shoulder. "They don't leave much to the imagination."

"Half the women in this town would kill for a derrière like yours." Sophia inspected her niece's slim figure admiringly. "Not to mention that flat tummy and tiny waist. You really were blessed at birth."

Misty remembered Brandon's words to that effect. If he thought she was attractive in her proper skirt and sweater, how would he react to these sexy pants? That made up her mind.

"Okay, you've convinced me. Now, what do I wear over them?"

Sophia had selected a variety of tops, all eye-catching in a different way. Some were sleeveless and daringly low cut. Others had demure necklines and long full sleeves, yet the sheer fabric revealed the body in a subtly erotic way.

Misty loved everything, but Sophia guided her shrewdly, passing up the ultraexpensive hand-beaded creations in favor of more reasonable tops that accomplished as striking an effect.

After taking Sophia's advice about including white satin pants and several skirts in her purchase, Misty had an extensive evening wardrobe.

"I can't believe I still have money left over after all this," she remarked happily while the saleswoman was wrapping her packages.

"We aren't through yet," Sophia warned. "You need daytime things, too."

Misty stopped buttoning her blouse. "Why didn't you remind me before I got dressed?"

"We don't have to pay these prices. I know a little discount house."

"I thought that was strictly an American phenomenon."

"We aren't the only ones who appreciate a bargain."

Sophia knew more than one discount house. She led Misty through all of them like a seasoned miner panning for gold, which she repeatedly uncovered.

"How can they sell things at these prices?" Misty was staring at a famous designer's label with disbelief.

"Some are samples, others are overruns or cancellations." Sophia was sorting intently through a rack of suits. "Too bad their evening selection isn't as extensive."

By the end of the afternoon Misty was outfitted like a jet-setter. She was also exhausted. When Sophia suggested stopping for a cappuccino at one of the sidewalk cafés on the Via Veneto, Misty agreed gratefully.

"I don't know how you do it." She slumped in her chair, gazing at her aunt's still-pristine appearance. "I look as though I'd been at a markdown sale of ten-dollar bills, and you don't have a hair out of place.''

"I wasn't trying on clothes."

"You were doing all the legwork, though. Why aren't you as bushed as I?"

Sophia laughed. "Years of rigorous training, darling."

"It certainly paid off. I never met anyone as knowledgeable about clothes," Misty said admiringly. "You can add another category to your list of possible vocations—personal shopper."

"That's a definite idea."

Misty paused, inspecting her aunt covertly while the waiter put foaming cups of cappuccino in front of them. Sophia looked as carefree as ever, but Misty wondered about the exact state of her finances. The fact that she'd put up only a feeble protest when Misty insisted on paying for her own wardrobe was rather ominous. She usually refused even to consider letting Misty pay for anything. Did that mean her aunt's juggling act was coming to an end?

"Are you really considering getting a job?" Misty asked quietly after the waiter had gone.

"Let's just say I'm available if anything challenging turns up," Sophia answered lightly.

Misty's fears were confirmed. "Your trouble is that you're too generous. We shouldn't be staying in a suite," she scolded. "You can't afford it."

"This is my last fling, and I intend to go out in style." Sophia smiled without a trace of sadness.

"Oh, Sophia, is it that bad?" Misty whispered.

"It isn't bad at all. I've had a wonderful life, and I anticipate many more good years." She smiled impishly.

"They might be spent in walk-up flats instead of luxury hotels, but I'm adaptable."

"You could come back to New York and share my apartment," Misty said haltingly. "I know it isn't what you're used to, but you wouldn't have any expenses, and you could take your time deciding what you want to do."

"That's a very generous offer, darling," Sophia said gently. "I'm touched."

"You'd really be doing me a favor," Misty said earnestly. "I'd love having you."

"I can't think of anyone I'd rather be with, but you mustn't worry about me. I always land on my feet." Sophia lifted her chin and inhaled the spring-scented air. "Who knows? Tomorrow a door might open on a fabulous new life."

"I hope so." Misty's voice was muted.

"Come on, let's go to the hairdresser. That will cheer you up."

It was typical of Sophia to worry about someone else's frame of mind. Misty decided the least she could do was try to match her consideration.

She pinned a smile on her face. "Okay, and let's go for the works."

"Now you're learning," Sophia said approvingly.

Alexander of the Ritz looked proudly at his handiwork after he'd finished with Misty's hair. He lifted it slightly in both hands.

"You see how I have layered the hair from underneath for fullness? Now it does not just hang to the shoulders. It billows out like a shining bell." He was overcome with admiration for his own skill.

Misty was delighted with the result. He had drawn back the hair at her temples and secured the two locks with a velvet bow, creating a ripple of curls in the back.

"You do look smashing, darling," Sophia agreed. "That violet eye shadow matches your eyes exactly, and I adore those contoured cheekbones. Rosella did a marvelous job."

Rosella was the makeup woman at the beauty salon. It was the first time Misty had ever had a professional makeup treatment. The result startled her, but she had to admit it was glamorous. Too bad Brandon couldn't see her that night. She'd never be able to duplicate any of this herself.

It was late by the time they returned to the hotel, but Sophia assured her they needn't rush.

"Bootsy's parties are like infinity," she said. "They have no beginning or end."

Misty stiffened. "Isn't she the blonde who was with Brandon last night?"

"That's the one."

"You didn't tell me it was *her* party."

"I didn't think it mattered." Sophia looked more closely at her niece. "Brandon takes her out, but she doesn't have any more claim on him than Jacqueline does."

"I couldn't care less," Misty remarked distantly.

"Good. I think you should play the field," Sophia answered innocently. "There will be dozens of eligible men there tonight."

Including Brandon? Misty wondered as she soaked in a bubble bath. Was Bootsy the real reason he hadn't asked to see her that evening? In spite of what Sophia said, the blonde's manner toward him had been very proprietary. But then, they *all* acted that way! Brandon clearly had the knack of making each woman think she was special to him.

Misty stood up abruptly and stepped out of the tub. She'd never been part of a harem, and she didn't intend to start now. Those other women were welcome to him! She took a quick look in the mirror at her new image to bolster her confidence.

"Eligible men, here I come," she muttered grimly.

The party was in full swing when they got to Bootsy's villa, an ancient mansion that had been completely refurbished. The large rooms flowed into each other, unified by a brown-veined, cream-colored marble floor buffed to a rich patina. Thick rugs broke up the vast expanse and added warmth to the rather austere atmosphere.

Beyond tall glass doors was a walled garden, glimpsed now and then through the crowds of people who gathered in groups and then dispersed like a restless school of fish.

All the guests, both men and women, were dressed in the height of fashion. Some of the more expensive designer creations looked almost like costumes. Misty was quietly amused that she'd thought her black satin pants too tight.

She'd worn the white ones instead, topped by a sleeveless white overblouse with a cowl neckline that dipped into a low V, front and back. Dangling pearl earrings were her only jewelry.

From the moment they arrived Misty received the rush Sophia had predicted. Men vied to dance with her, to bring her champagne, to get her something to eat. It was a heady experience. She whirled from one man to another until it was impossible to remember all their names. Once, unexpectedly, she found herself in Clark's arms.

"You're the hit of the party," he commented. "It wasn't easy to get a dance with you."

"I suppose I'm a novelty. These people see each other all the time," she said dismissively. "How are you, Clark? I didn't know you were going to be here tonight."

"Bootsy isn't particular about whom she invites," he answered sardonically. "She just likes to fill up the place with warm bodies."

"I suppose that includes me," Misty said. "I don't even know her."

"Don't worry, you're welcome as long as you don't try to make off with her main man."

"Who would that be?" Misty asked, although she already knew the answer.

"Brandon Powers. She's crazy about him. They all are," Clark said with ill-concealed envy.

"Is he here tonight?" Misty kept her voice casual.

"I haven't seen him, but he'll probably turn up." Clark snickered. "Even if it's not until everyone's gone."

Misty was glad when a man named Duane Creighton cut in.

"You can't monopolize this beautiful lady," he said.

"I have more right than you do. You don't even know her name," said Clark, sneering.

"No, but I'm going to. Go decorate a room, Clark." Duane smiled down at her, dismissing the other man without a glance.

After Clark had relinquished her and moved away, Misty said, "That wasn't very nice." She was glad to be rid of him, though.

Duane laughed. "Everyone kids old Clark. He doesn't mind." His embrace tightened. "But why are we talking about him? *You're* the object of my desire. Tell me all your hopes and dreams."

"I'd rather hear about yours."

"You figure prominently in them," he answered in a throaty voice.

Misty smiled. This was like being back in college. "You don't know anything about me. I could be a dangerous foreign agent."

"I'll talk! Come to my apartment, and I'll tell you everything." Duane fended off an attempt to cut in. "Go away. Can't you see this beautiful spy and I are exchanging secrets?"

"Is this man bothering you, miss?" The newcomer pretended to slap Duane's cheek. "I challenge you to a duel, sir. Your choice of weapons."

Duane frowned thoughtfully. "Decisions, always decisions. I can never decide between martinis or manhattans."

"What's the difference? They're both lethal," the other man said.

Misty was laughing at their nonsense when she saw Brandon across the room. He was standing in the doorway watching her. When their eyes met he started toward her.

As she watched him make his way with catlike grace through the crowded room, Misty's heart began to thunder. What was there about him that affected her this way? The men she was with were both tall and good-looking. They were self-assured and amusing, but they didn't have Brandon's indefinable something. Maybe it was chemistry—or just maybe it was something else.

"What did you do to yourself?" He took both of her hands. "You look beautiful."

"I had my hair done," she murmured.

"*Beautiful* wasn't the right word. Tonight you're exquisite." The pressure of his hands increased.

"Wouldn't you know Brandon got to her first?" Duane groaned.

"We outnumber him," his friend said. "How about settling this in a fair fight? You hold him, and I'll hit him."

"Go somewhere else and play, boys." Brandon folded her in his arms. "Misty and I want to be alone."

They danced in silence for a few minutes. Misty was content just to be near him, to inhale his subtle male scent, to feel the play of muscles as his thighs brushed hers. Until the slow movement of his body against hers began to overwhelm her.

She drew away slightly. "Is your friend here with you tonight?"

"Who?" He looked at her blankly.

"The one you went to meet at the airport."

"Oh...Jim. No, he was suffering from jet lag, so I dropped him off at his hotel."

"Too bad. He's missing a nice party."

Brandon's expression was sardonic as he looked over the crowd in their glittering clothes and jewels. "There will be others."

"I suppose so," Misty murmured. Why could she banter so easily with other men, but not with Brandon?

His eyes warmed as they turned to her. "What did you do today after I left you?"

"Sophia and I went shopping."

"Is this one of your purchases?" He held her at arm's length and looked her up and down admiringly. "It's fantastic! But then, you always look like a dream come true.'' He drew her close again.

''Is that what you tell Bootsy and Jacqueline and all the rest?'' She tried to keep her tone light.

''Why would you think that?''

''Because it's too good a line to be used on only one woman.''

He chuckled richly. ''You don't credit me with much imagination.''

Misty had hoped for a denial. ''You don't need imagination; you need stamina,'' she answered coolly.

Brandon struggled to contain his amusement. ''I have plenty of that, as you'd find out if you'd be a little more cooperative.''

She tilted her head back to look up at him indignantly. ''Is that supposed to be a recommendation?''

''Surely you don't want testimonial letters?'' he teased.

''I don't want *anything* from you,'' she snapped.

''That's too bad, because I want a great deal from you.'' His lips brushed her temple. ''I'd like to take you to bed for a week.''

She ignored the mind-boggling images his statement conjured up. ''That sounds ambitious, even for you.''

''Try me.'' He smiled.

''Do you give a money-back guarantee?'' she asked a little breathlessly.

''I'll do more than that.'' His warm breath tantalized her ear. ''I'll give you a replacement service if you're not completely satisfied.''

''That's a pretty tall promise from a man who has yet to ask me out on a date.''

''How about tomorrow night?''

''You see? It's never your idea.'' Frustration filled her voice.

A tender look crossed his face as he gazed down at her. "Sweet little Misty, you wouldn't believe the ideas I've had about you."

"No, I wouldn't."

His muted, husky voice almost accomplished its purpose. Brandon could convince a bird to give up flying. But that didn't alter the facts.

"I'd spend every minute with you if I could, sweetheart, but I happen to have...other commitments."

"Yes, I know. At least one blonde and one redhead," Misty said waspishly.

A slow smile spread over his face. "Jealousy is a very positive sign."

"Don't flatter yourself! Your sex life is of no interest to me."

"It isn't as lurid as you imagine."

Misty frowned in annoyance. "I wish you'd pick one side and stick to it. First you tell me how sensational you are in bed, and then you imply that you're practically celibate."

He grinned. "Which would you prefer?"

"How can I convince you that I don't care? But I don't believe for one minute that you're celibate," she couldn't help adding.

"How about you?" he asked unexpectedly. "How many men have there been?"

"I don't... That's none of your business," she sputtered.

"You feel free to discuss *my* sex life."

"That's different! I mean, you're..." Her voice trailed off. "No, you have a valid point. I have no right to censure you. We're practically strangers."

"I wouldn't say that," he murmured. "I know a lot about you—the perfume you wear, the way your lips taste, the contours of your beautiful body." His hand moved sensuously over her waist. "And I'm going to know more."

Nervous laughter welled up in her throat. "You seem to have learned a lot about me already."

"I'm missing one important fact."

"I don't care to know what it is," she said hurriedly.

He told her anyway. "I want to know how it feels to wake up with you curled in my arms after a night of love."

"It wouldn't be a novel experience for you," she said weakly.

"With you it would be." Tiny pinpoints of light flickered in his eyes as he gazed down at her almost perfect features. "I've never met anyone quite like you—part wide-eyed teenager, part seductive woman. Whoever you are, my little love, you're totally enchanting."

The smoldering desire on his face turned her liquid inside. She was gazing up at him wordlessly when their hostess joined them, bringing Misty back to earth. Brandon promptly released her.

"Someone told me you were here," Bootsy said to Brandon. "You might have had the courtesy to say hello."

"I apologize for my bad manners," he answered evenly.

"What kept you?" she demanded.

"I wasn't aware that I had a deadline." His smile didn't reach his eyes.

Bootsy was immediately conciliatory. "I missed you," she said softly.

Brandon glanced around the crowded room. "You would seem to have had your hands full without me." He brought Misty into the conversation, since Bootsy showed no inclination to do so. "You've met Sophia's niece, of course."

"Yes." Her appraising glance was flinty.

"It was so nice of you to have me," Misty said politely. "Your home is beautiful."

Clark joined them before the other woman could reply. "Wonderful party, Bootsy."

"It is now." Her glance at Brandon was sultry.

"You always give the best parties in Rome," Clark gushed.

"That's what you told Mimi Fontelli at *her* party," she answered mockingly. "If you must be a toady, Clark, at least try to be original."

"Excuse me," Misty murmured, backing away as his face turned a dull red.

Clark might be a wimp, but Bootsy's manners were inexcusable. She was obviously used to saying exactly what she pleased, no matter how cutting—except to Brandon. He had apparently made it clear that sleeping with her didn't include taking her abuse.

Misty found Sophia talking to an interesting-looking older man. He was almost as tall as Brandon but not as magnificently trim. The years had taken their toll, and his still impressive physique was lightly cushioned now. His face had gained character, however.

Laughter lines rayed out from gray eyes that were nonetheless piercing, and his mouth had a no-nonsense firmness to it. His personality evidently matched his impressive appearance, because Sophia's face was animated.

She beckoned to Misty. "I want you to meet Warren Dillingham, darling. He's in the oil business in Texas. My niece, Misty Carlysle."

After acknowledging the introduction, Warren looked curiously at Misty. "There isn't any family resemblance between you, is there?"

Sophia smiled. "Unfortunately not. Misty is the beauty in the family."

"Not the only one," he answered gallantly.

"What part of Texas are you from, Mr. Dillingham?" Misty asked.

"Warren, please, and I'm from Houston."

"You don't sound like a Texan," she observed.

"That's because I went away to school during my early years. When I'm back home, though, I find myself slipping into a southern drawl." As though to illustrate the point, his words became slightly slurred.

"I think a southern accent is charming," Sophia remarked.

"But not nearly as polished sounding as these folks." He indicated the stylish guests.

Sophia laughed. "These folks are predominantly American. Poor Misty. I promised her dukes and earls, and all she's met so far are her own countrymen."

"You're looking for titles?" Warren asked Misty.

"Only as a spectator sport," she assured him. "Royalty is in short supply in New York."

"Don't be discouraged, pet," Sophia said. "We just arrived. How long have you been in Rome?" she asked Warren.

"Not long," he answered.

"Are you here for business or pleasure?"

"Pleasure, definitely. I'm a tired businessman seeking relaxation."

"I don't know if you came to the right place," Sophia said wryly. "Rome is pretty frenetic."

"Do they party like this every night?"

Sophia shrugged. "You know Bootsy's crowd."

"Who?"

"Our hostess."

Warren looked uncomfortable. "Well, actually, I don't really know the lady. I'm a friend of a friend."

"Join the group," Misty said sardonically. "I'm here under false pretenses, too."

"I didn't mean to imply—"

"Neither of you need to feel that way," Sophia interposed. "Bootsy likes to play with a full house. The more the merrier."

Misty made a face. "Clark called us warm bodies, which is probably closer to the truth."

Warren's expression was unreadable. "You mean anyone can crash these parties?"

"I suppose if they have enough nerve," Sophia said.

"That doesn't sound very prudent," he remarked. "There are a lot of unsavory people just waiting to prey on the rich."

"Confidence men?" Sophia laughed. "First you have to get their attention."

"I was thinking of thieves. The jewelry here tonight is quite impressive."

"I suppose that could be tempting, but the continent's been plagued with cat burglars, not holdup men."

"They'd find slim pickings if you ladies would keep your jewels in the hotel safe."

"It's such a nuisance to go through the whole procedure every time you want to put something in or take it out. Especially after a party, when one's tired."

"Isn't it better than losing your possessions?"

"I suppose no one ever believes she'll be a victim."

"That kind of thinking keeps the criminal world in business," Warren said dryly.

"The scariest part is the thought of someone coming into your room while you're asleep." Misty shivered.

"Cat burglars aren't violent," Sophia reassured her.

"The potential for violence is always there," he warned. "I hope you're taking proper precautions. That necklace you're wearing is magnificent."

Sophia slanted an amused glance at Misty. "I don't think we're in any danger from a jewel thief."

"You have connections to the underworld?" Warren asked casually.

"Hardly. I just meant that Misty and I are very cautious."

"One of us more than the other," Misty observed a little tartly.

"Life wasn't meant to be played safe," her aunt protested. "That takes all the fun out of it. Don't you agree?" she asked Warren. "Your business involves risk, doesn't it?"

He smiled. "More than you know, my dear."

"You wouldn't trade it for a desk job, though, would you?"

"I'm required to spend more time than I like at a desk, regrettably." He patted his abdomen. "As you can tell."

"Not at all. You're extremely athletic looking. I'll bet you play tennis."

"Golf," he corrected. "At least when I get the chance. What do you do to keep that stunning figure?"

"Self-denial," Sophia answered ruefully. "Like everyone else. As you can see, there isn't a fat person in sight."

"You can never be too rich or too thin?" he asked in a faintly derisive tone.

"That's the prevailing opinion."

"Not with me," Misty said. "The food here is too fantastic."

"You'll have to recommend some restaurants," he said. "I have no idea where to go."

"Are you here all alone?" Sophia asked.

"Yes, that's why I accepted this invitation when it came along."

"Who is the friend who brought you?"

"Someone I don't even know very well." He smiled appealingly. "That gives you some idea of how lonely I am."

"You won't be after tonight," she said soothingly. "I'll see that you meet all the right people."

"I already have," he murmured with a special inflection.

Misty decided her presence was no longer required. She was about to excuse herself when Brandon joined them.

"You're looking radiant as always, Sophia." Brandon's eyes traveled from her face to her sparkling necklace.

"You're a dear," she answered. "But what about Misty? Doesn't she look smashing?"

Brandon put his arm around Misty's shoulders. "I've already told her so. In fact, I fought my way through a host of admirers to do it."

Sophia looked gratified. "Have you met Warren Dillingham? He's just arrived in Rome."

The two men shook hands and exchanged conventional remarks. It was an ordinary social ritual, but Misty had the fleeting impression that they'd met before. A flash of recognition seemed to pass between them as their eyes met. Since they would have no reason to deny knowing each other, Misty decided she must be mistaken.

The conversation was predictable. Brandon asked Warren where he was from and answered a couple of questions on his own background. Then they discussed Rome and its attractions.

"Misty is the one to advise you about that." Brandon laughed. "She has a list a mile long of things to see."

"You're welcome to come with me," Misty told Warren. "Sophia isn't interested, and Brandon just pretends to enjoy himself."

"You know better than that," Brandon reproached her.

"And what makes you think I wouldn't enjoy coming along?" Sophia asked. "I think it would be great fun if the four of us made a day of it. I know an adorable inn just outside of Rome. We could drive out and have lunch."

"Is that your idea of sight-seeing?" Misty asked.

"Why not? It's a site, and you've never seen it before," she replied airily. "A place doesn't have to be an ancient ruin to be interesting."

"Stick with Sophia, and you'll know every eating place within a radius of fifty miles," Misty told Warren.

"If you insist on antiquities, I dare say we can find some antique shops along the way," Sophia said.

"It sounds most enjoyable," Warren said. "How about tomorrow?"

"That would be lovely." Sophia accepted promptly.

"Excellent." Warren looked inquiringly at Brandon.

"Sounds good to me, too," he said. "Now all we have to do is convince the little sightseer."

Misty didn't need any convincing to spend a day with Brandon, but she didn't want him to know how eager she was. "Okay," she answered tepidly. "I suppose the drive out will be scenic anyway."

"Good, then if it's all settled, I'm going to take Warren around and introduce him to some people," Sophia said.

"I suppose I should meet my hostess," he agreed. "I'm ashamed to say I don't even know what she looks like."

Sophia scanned the crowded room. "There she is. The blonde in the black dress dancing with the man with the little mustache."

As they all automatically followed her direction, Misty was amazed to see that the man was Clark. He was not only dancing with Bootsy, he was fawning over her.

"I can't believe what I'm seeing," Misty murmured to Brandon. "Clark must be a glutton for punishment. If she'd ever talked to *me* like that, I'd have walked away and kept on going."

Brandon's expression was cynical as he watched the other couple. Clark was talking eagerly, while Bootsy looked bored.

"Maybe he's trying to sell her on remodeling the villa."

"There must be easier ways to make money," Misty answered sharply.

Brandon shrugged. "If you want big money, you put up with big annoyances."

That might explain Clark's demeaning behavior, but it didn't explain Brandon's attraction to Bootsy. *He* didn't stand to gain anything from her. Or did he? Was he really playing an elaborate charade? Misty wanted to reject the idea as ridiculous, but so many of Brandon's actions were incomprehensible.

"I'd better go break them up before Bootsy unsheathes her claws again." His amused voice broke in on Misty's troubled thoughts.

She watched the blonde's expression become animated as she turned away from Clark. Bootsy was a different woman in Brandon's arms. Her boredom was replaced by warmth and seduction.

Clark was well aware of the transformation. Powerful emotions warred on his face as he walked away: anger, frustration—and something else not as easily definable.

Misty couldn't help feeling sorry for him. He was so tied up in knots that he didn't even see her until they almost collided.

"Sorry," he muttered. "I wasn't looking where I was going."

"It's awfully crowded in here," she said gently.

"Yes, it is." He stared at her intently for a moment. "Let's go out in the garden and get a breath of fresh air."

"Well, I—"

She didn't really want to be alone with him, but Clark's hand was firm on her arm. Misty sighed inwardly. He was probably the lesser of two evils. She didn't want to watch Brandon dancing with Bootsy, either.

The garden was surrounded by a high brick wall with a grillwork gate that led to the sidewalk. Masses of flowers were only pale shapes in the darkness, but their scent perfumed the air.

Misty sank down on a scrolled bench and took a deep breath. "It's lovely out here."

"And quieter," Clark answered grimly.

"Scusi." Another guest had followed them out of the house, a dark-haired man of medium height. He was apparently leaving, but he paused by the gate, patting his pockets. "Do you have a match?" he asked.

Clark walked over to him and took a packet of matches out of his jacket. "You can keep them," he said.

"Grazie." The man bowed slightly in Misty's direction. *"Addio, signorina."*

After the gate clicked behind him she said, "Italian is such a romantic language, isn't it?"

"I suppose so," Clark answered indifferently.

"Their manners are beautiful, too. Did you know that man?"

"Just slightly."

"What's his name?"

"Count Passorini or Passetori—something like that."

"I'll have to tell Sophia I finally met a real live count! Or at least saw one, anyway."

"Rome is full of them." Clark shrugged. "Most of them don't have one nickel to rub against another."

"But think what a long, noble lineage they have."

"Filled with wastrels and conspirators. If those guys were alive today, they'd either be in prison or politics." Clark's smile was unpleasant.

Misty understood why he was in such a foul mood, but her patience was dwindling. Clark made it difficult to sustain compassion. She was about to suggest they go back inside when a commotion arose in the house.

The noise level of the party had been high, but this was different. The raised voices held an undertone of urgency.

"I wonder what's going on," Misty said.

"Maybe Bootsy poisoned the punch."

"We'd better see what's happening."

"Sure, we wouldn't want to miss the entertainment." Clark's mouth curved mockingly.

Chapter Five

All the guests were clustered in little groups when Misty and Clark reentered the house. The music had stopped, and everyone was talking earnestly while scanning the floor. A few people were bent over for a closer look. Misty started toward her aunt, who was still with Warren.

"Why is everyone standing around?" she asked.

"Bootsy lost her ring," Sophia said.

"That huge diamond?"

"Yes, it was a flawless stone."

"You mean it fell out of the setting?" Misty asked.

"No, the ring itself is missing."

Misty stared at her blankly. "How can you lose something that's on your finger?"

"There's always the possibility that it slipped off," Warren said. "Everyone's been looking for it."

"A diamond that size shouldn't be hard to find," Misty remarked.

"If it was lost, that is," he said quietly.

"You don't think it was stolen!" She turned a shocked face to him. "How could anyone take it without her knowledge?"

"It wouldn't be that difficult," Sophia answered thoughtfully. "People are always squeezing hands while they exchange those social kisses."

"I can't believe one of her own guests would do such a thing," Misty said helplessly.

"It isn't a pleasant thought," Warren agreed.

"You think it's possible, though."

His face was expressionless. "It's one explanation."

Bootsy's raised voice commanded everyone's attention. "Listen to me, all of you! If I don't get my ring back, there's going to be plenty of hell to pay around here. No lousy thief rips me off and gets away with it!"

Clark pushed his way through the circle around her, which included Brandon. "Bravo! I say we should all submit to a search."

Brandon looked at him unemotionally. "You think that would produce the ring?"

"If somebody here took it."

"Very neat." Brandon smiled derisively. "The thief has the loot in a pocket or purse, just waiting to be discovered."

"What else would he do with it?" Clark demanded.

"I wonder," Brandon mused.

"So do I," Clark answered pugnaciously. "You were the last person to dance with Bootsy. Does that have anything to do with your objection to being searched?"

Brandon ignored the little gasps all around them. "I didn't say I objected, just that it wouldn't do any good."

"And I say an innocent person has nothing to lose. How about it, Powers?" Clark sneered. "Are you willing to put your money where your mouth is?"

Brandon's smile was mocking. "Will the contents of my pockets satisfy you, or do you demand a strip search?"

"Don't be ridiculous, Clark," Bootsy said impatiently. "I don't suspect Brandon."

"Maybe you should," he muttered furiously. "Just remember, I was the one who suggested everybody be searched. And I still think it's a good idea."

She looked over his shoulder. "Thank God the police are here. Maybe now we'll get someplace."

The police took everyone's name and address. They examined the premises and asked a lot of carefully phrased questions, but the subject of a search never arose.

Clark was coldly furious that his suggestion wasn't considered. He made quite a nuisance of himself, pointing out the way *he* would have handled the investigation.

When the police were finished with them, the party was effectively over. All the guests left hurriedly after murmured sympathies to their hostess.

In the taxi going back to the hotel, Warren said to Brandon, "That Foster fellow doesn't seem to care much for you."

"He was sulking because of something nasty Bootsy said to him earlier," Misty explained.

"In that case, it's strange that he wanted to turn the place upside down after the theft," Warren remarked.

"You showed remarkable forbearance," Sophia told Brandon. "A lesser man might have flattened Clark—with good cause."

Brandon's face was unreadable in the darkness, but his tone was relaxed. "He was just having his moment of glory."

"At your expense!" Misty declared indignantly. "I agree with Sophia. You should have belted him one."

"Don't you think we had enough excitement at the party?"

"What happened tonight was truly shocking," Sophia said. "Cat burglars are bad enough, but when these people invade a private party, it's really rather frightening."

Misty intercepted a glance between the two men that sent a tiny chill up her spine. Perhaps it was just the shifting shadows in the cab, but for just a moment their faces looked hard. With the mask of geniality stripped away, they seemed formidable somehow.

Misty fell silent as the conversation flowed around her. She remembered her earlier feeling that Brandon and Warren had met before. Was Warren who he said he was? For that matter, was Brandon? Clark's accusation echoed in Misty's ears. Brandon *had* been the last one to dance with Bootsy, and she was so infatuated with him that she wouldn't have noticed if he'd slipped the ring off her finger.

Misty even thought she knew how it could be done. One seductive hand moving over her back, his warm breath feathering her ear as he murmured sensuous suggestions. A woman's attention would be distracted under a siege like that.

When the taxi dropped them off at their hotel, Warren said, "Would anyone care for a nightcap?"

Misty shook her head. "Not for me, thanks, but you go ahead, Sophia."

"No, I'm rather tired, too. It's been an eventful evening."

"I'll see you both tomorrow, then. You, too, Brandon. We have a date, right?"

"I'm looking forward to it," Sophia answered. As they walked to the elevator she remarked, "Isn't it convenient that we're all staying at the same hotel?"

Brandon gave Misty a special smile. "Just lucky, I guess."

When they were in their suite Sophia gave Misty a concerned look. "You were very quiet in the cab. Do you feel all right?"

"I'm fine. I was just . . . thinking."

"About what?"

Misty hesitated. "You spent quite a bit of time with Warren. Did you find out any more about him?"

Sophia smiled mischievously. "I found out the most important thing. He isn't married. He's marvelously attractive, wouldn't you say?"

"Yes," Misty answered doubtfully.

Her aunt was quick to catch the reservation in her voice. "Didn't you like him? You don't want to go tomorrow, is that it?"

"No, it sounds like fun."

"Then what's this all about? I know when something's troubling you, pet."

Misty shrugged. "Maybe it was the robbery tonight that made me feel creepy. The thought that someone there was a thief. It makes you start to suspect everyone."

"The police would have appreciated any suggestions," Sophia said dryly. "Whom do you suspect?"

"No one, actually. I was just— How do you know Warren is a big oilman from Texas?" Misty asked abruptly.

"I can't believe this! Why on earth would you think Warren is a suspicious character?"

"For one thing, he doesn't sound like any Texan *I've* ever met."

"He explained that," Sophia replied impatiently.

"Maybe."

"You're letting your imagination run away with you. I told you to be careful, not paranoid!"

"Why won't you admit he could be something other than he seems?"

"Anybody could. I'm a good example of that," Sophia pointed out. "But you're way off base about Warren. He never went near Bootsy. He was with me the entire time."

Her aunt's statement didn't make Misty feel a lot better. It left Brandon as the prime suspect.

Sophia examined her niece's clouded face. "I'm a good judge of character—in spite of Clark." She laughed. "Anyone's entitled to one mistake. But take my word for it, we've found two winners."

"I hope so," Misty answered soberly.

The bright sunlight streaming through the windows the next morning improved Misty's mood. She decided that her uneasiness the night before had been due to nerves. The party had ended on a decidedly unpleasant note. Today would make up for it, though.

Since they wouldn't be walking around the cobblestone streets, she wore high heels with a silk dress that was softly feminine.

"You look adorable, pet," Sophia said when they were ready to leave. "The violets in that print are the exact color of your eyes."

"You look great, too," Misty replied.

Sophia had on a white silk suit that was quietly elegant. She had chosen not to accessorize its simple lines and wore only small gold earrings and an emerald ring.

The men were openly admiring when they all met in the lobby.

"I hope this inn we're going to is suitably plush for two such lovely ladies," Warren said gallantly.

"You'll adore it," Sophia assured him. "It's an idyllic spot. We can have lunch on the terrace overlooking vineyards and a charming little lake."

"How far is it?" Misty asked.

"Less than an hour's drive."

"The way Italians drive, or the way sane people do?" Brandon grinned.

Misty groaned. "I might make the entire trip with my eyes closed."

"I won't be able to help you this time," he teased. "I'm driving."

Misty's color rose as she remembered the method Brandon had used to distract her in the taxi.

"Shall we get started?" Warren suggested.

The drive through the countryside was beautiful, and less traumatic than the city streets. Blaring horns and congestion gave way to bird songs coming from tall trees that shaded the landscape.

Set well back from the road were imposing villas surrounded by extensive grounds. Many of the houses looked at least a century old, but they were impeccably maintained.

"It's so peaceful here compared to the city," Misty remarked, gazing at a winding driveway bordered by stately poplars.

"I suppose that's why people move to the suburbs," Sophia commented.

"These aren't exactly tract houses," Misty replied dryly.

"They're still out in the country," Sophia said.

"I gather you don't care for suburbia," Warren remarked.

"I wouldn't say that. I've had some fabulous times at house parties."

His mouth curved cynically. "In other words, it's a nice place to visit, but you wouldn't want to live there."

"That's not what I meant at all," she protested. "The place doesn't matter. It's whom you share it with."

Warren's voice softened. "Yes, it's lonely living by yourself."

Sophia nodded. "That's why I'm so happy to have Misty here. She's like a daughter to me."

"More like a sister." Misty gazed fondly at her glamorous aunt.

Warren looked at her with equal admiration. "It's difficult to believe you're not married. Although I know it's by choice," he added hurriedly.

"Not really. I'm a widow," she said quietly.

"I'm sorry." His voice was gentle as he saw the expression in her eyes.

"How about you?" Sophia smiled, banishing her sadness. "I could return the compliment by asking how such a handsome man escaped matrimony."

"We share a common bond. My wife died many years ago. I'm fortunate to have a family, though, three grown children. My middle boy is about Misty's age."

"If you're thinking of making a match, forget it," Brandon warned. "She's spoken for."

"A woman has to look to the future," Misty joked. "I'll be going home eventually. Where does your son live?"

"In Philadelphia like . . . my other two children."

Warren's slight hesitation went unnoticed except by Brandon. The eyes of the two men met in the rearview mirror, but Brandon didn't make any comment.

"That's your hometown," Misty said to Brandon. "Do you know Warren's son?"

He shook his head. "I haven't spent much time in Philadelphia the last few years."

"It's sad that your family lives so far away," Sophia said to Warren. "Have you ever considered moving east?"

"I've thought about it now and then." He glanced out the window at an imposing estate surrounded by a grill-work fence. "How about *that* house? It must belong to one of those princes Misty's trying to track down."

"I'm not doing too well," she said. "So far I've only seen one count, and all he did was bow in my direction. I didn't even get my hand kissed."

"Where was this?" Sophia asked.

"At the party last night when I was out in the garden with Clark."

"The man clearly had no class. What was his name?" Brandon asked casually.

"I don't know. Clark wasn't sure. He said he only knew him slightly."

"How unlike Foster not to pursue the friendship." Brandon's voice was mocking.

"He must not have had any money," Misty agreed.

"Let's not discuss that tiresome little man," Sophia said.

They reached the inn a few minutes later, and it was all Sophia had promised. The mellowed brick building was set on a hilltop overlooking a picturesque lake that had black and white swans floating regally on its glassy surface, like mobile statues. A lush green lawn sloped down to the water, bordered on either side by leafy vineyards.

They had lunch on a flagstone terrace under a brightly hued umbrella. Large pots of pink and red geraniums on a low retaining wall added spots of color that attracted tiny, darting hummingbirds.

The food was as perfect as the setting. They began with a salad of sweet red peppers bathed in *bagna cauda*, a rich dressing flavored with garlic and anchovies.

The main course was baby lamb chops coated in parmesan cheese and browned in butter. They were served with mushrooms and tiny green peas sprinkled with fresh mint. Adding to the enjoyment was the presentation. Each plate was like a picture out of a magazine.

Misty sighed ecstatically. "I don't know where I'm putting all of this, but I'm loving every bite."

"Save room for dessert," Sophia advised.

"You have to be kidding!"

"No, they make an absolutely divine *cassata gelata*."

Brandon grinned. "It sounds like an Italian motel."

"*Gelata* is ice cream," Misty informed him loftily. "Even I know that."

"But this is like none you've ever tasted," Sophia said. "It's crammed with candied fruit and sugared nuts."

"Are you going to have some, too?" Warren asked.

"Of course."

"I thought you said you kept your figure through self-denial."

"Rules are made to be broken," she answered lightly.

He gazed at her appraisingly. "If you can get away with it, that is."

Sophia laughed. "Naturally. There's no point if you have to pay the consequences."

"I'm one of those unfortunates," Brandon remarked. "I might have to jog around the lake a couple of times to work off this lunch." He looked at Misty. "How about it? Are you with me?"

"Not in these shoes. I'll just sit here and applaud your performance."

"I don't demand applause, only cooperation," he murmured.

Misty's cheeks turned a becoming pink at his suggestive tone. She knew Brandon wasn't talking about jogging. At least Sophia and Warren weren't listening. They were having a discussion of their own.

"No comment?" Brandon teased, aware of her quick glance at the other couple.

"You don't want cooperation; you want surrender," she replied in a low voice.

"You're wrong, angel. It will only be good if we're equal partners."

Although he'd kept his voice as low as hers, Misty shot a nervous look at her aunt and Warren. "We'll discuss it later," she said hurriedly.

He laughed. "I must be making progress. This is the first time you haven't turned me down flat."

His laughter attracted Sophia's attention. "Are we missing something?"

"No," Misty answered grimly.

"How do you know?" Brandon asked softly.

She pushed her chair back. "Excuse me. I'm going to the powder room."

"I'll go with you." Her aunt stood up, also.

When they were alone, Sophia said, "Are you enjoying yourself, pet?"

"Yes, the lunch was fabulous. It would be worth the drive even if the scenery weren't so spectacular."

"I thought it would be something different to do."

"What's the name of this place? I want to write it down in my trip diary."

"It's called Los Cignos—that's *the swans*, in Italian."

"Aren't they lovely? The whole setting is," Misty said. "I'd like to walk down to the lake before we start back."

Her aunt nodded. "We aren't in any hurry. That's the beauty of this spot. People come here to relax and unwind."

"How did you ever hear about it?"

"An Italian friend of mine spent her honeymoon here. They only had a few days, and they didn't want to waste time flying to some resort."

"You mean this really is a hotel? I thought it was just a restaurant."

"It's an inn rather than a hotel. They only have about ten rooms. Gina said they were charming, but who can trust the observation of a woman on her honeymoon?" Sophia laughed.

"I imagine she's right, though. Everything is so well kept up. I wouldn't mind spending a few days here."

Sophia's eyes sparkled mischievously. "Don't say that in front of Brandon or you'll find your wish granted."

"He wouldn't last for more than one day." Misty took a comb out of her purse and concentrated on combing her already smooth hair.

Sophia looked at her niece's set face with amusement. "I think you're seriously underestimating the man."

"I meant his attention span," Misty replied curtly. "Brandon is the sort of man who requires quantity."

"I'm sure he's more selective than that," Sophia protested.

"You make a lot of allowances for people you like," Misty muttered.

"Isn't that the way it should be?"

"I suppose so, but you persist in ignoring the facts."

"You haven't given me any—just innuendoes. Like those ridiculous suspicions of Warren. I trust you've changed your mind about him after today."

"He's very charming," Misty admitted grudgingly.

"That sounds as though you *haven't* changed your mind." Sophia looked at her impatiently. "The poor man is a lonely widower on vacation, not an international spy, for heaven's sake!"

"I never said he was a spy."

"All right, a jewel thief, then. That's almost as bad."

"I didn't say that, either. I merely raised the possibility."

"And I told you it was an *im*possibility!" Sophia answered heatedly. "It was just a coincidence that he happened to be at that party in the first place."

"Did you ever find out who the friend was who brought him?"

"I saw no reason to give him the third degree. Warren has been very open about himself. Unless you think he made up a dead wife and three grown sons," Sophia added sarcastically.

"Maybe he supported them by lifting little baubles here and there," Misty joked.

She didn't really suspect Warren of being a jewel thief, but she did have a feeling that he wasn't being completely honest with them for some reason.

Sophia failed to see the humor in her remark. "If you feel that way, I don't see how you could have accepted his hospitality today."

Her aunt's impassioned defense of Warren was uncharacteristic. Sophia didn't usually argue a point heatedly, nor did she ever get this waspish.

"You like Warren a lot, don't you?" Misty asked slowly.

The thin line of Sophia's mouth softened. "Yes, very much," she said quietly. "There was an instant rapport between us."

The underlying intensity in her aunt's voice made Misty vaguely uneasy. In spite of her sophistication, Sophia could get hurt like any other woman. What if Warren wasn't a widower? That could be what he was hiding. He could have a wife at home who thought he was off on a business trip. It would be fruitless to point that out to Sophia, though. She was sold on the man.

Misty hid her fears behind a smile. "You always were a pushover for a stray. Warren was wandering around like a lost soul, and you took him under your wing."

Sophia returned her smile. "I like to think it was kismet."

That's what Brandon had said about *their* meeting. Wouldn't it be nice if there were something to preordination after all? Misty thought wistfully.

She stood up. "We'd better get back. They'll be wondering what happened to us."

As Sophia rose and straightened her jacket, she uttered an annoyed exclamation. "I have a spot on my sleeve."

Misty inspected the small red stain. "It looks like wine. You'd better put cold water on it right away."

"Or it will never come out," Sophia agreed. "Go on without me, pet. I'll be along in a couple of minutes."

Misty decided to take a shortcut across the lawn. They had really been gone quite a long time. She had almost reached the terrace when her high heel caught in a hidden sprinkler head. She stumbled, and her purse sailed into the thick bushes directly under the terrace.

Misty was annoyed to discover that all the contents had spilled out. As she crawled into the greenery trying to retrieve her possessions, the voices of the two men floated down to her. She was about to call out for assistance when the import of their words registered.

"You really have to be more careful," Brandon was saying. "It's the little things that trip you up."

"I'm not a professional like you," Warren answered apologetically.

"That's why it would have been better not to become personally involved."

The older man's voice hardened. "Quite a lot of money is at stake."

"That's what you have me for." Brandon sounded impatient.

"I can be helpful. You were right about Sophia. She does know everyone worth knowing."

"And she can open a lot of doors. Just be careful. She's one shrewd lady."

"Not the way you think." Warren sounded discontented. "I really can't agree with you there."

"I know how you feel. She's a fascinating woman. But we can't afford to take any chances."

Misty's heart was pounding furiously. All her vague suspicions were true! Brandon and Warren were criminals. As if that weren't bad enough, they were planning to involve Sophia! Anger and indignation warred with deep regret inside her. She should have known Brandon was too good to be true.

Sophia had to be warned. But would she listen? Or would she say Misty had misinterpreted what she'd heard? A woman attracted that powerfully to a man often believed what she wanted to believe.

Misty set her chin grimly. The first thing to do was have a little chat with Brandon. If she couldn't talk sense into her aunt, she'd have to tell Brandon he'd been found out. Sophia would be unhappy when Warren dropped her, but it was better than waiting until she was really in love with him.

Misty crept out from under the bushes and made her way cautiously toward the terrace, staying close to the shrubbery. When she arrived at the table, her aunt was already there.

"Where on earth have you been?" Sophia asked.

"I, uh, I stopped to look at the flowers."

Brandon plucked a leaf from her disheveled hair. "You look as though you've been rolling in them."

"They're beautiful." Misty's grim expression was at odds with her words. "Come with me and see for yourself."

"The waiter is bringing dessert," Sophia objected.

"Tell him to save ours till later," Misty ordered.

After a puzzled look at her set face Brandon said, "These must be pretty special flowers. I can't wait to see them."

She didn't say anything until they were out of sight of the other two, but the effort made her breathing rapid.

"Is something the matter?" Brandon asked after she'd answered all of his remarks in monosyllables.

"You bet there is! I know everything," she said dramatically.

He chuckled. "That's quite a feat. I wish I did."

"Don't try to pretend you don't know what I mean. I heard you and Warren talking."

Brandon's laughter stilled. "What did you hear?" he asked casually.

"You know perfectly well! I won't go into the morality of the thing, because you obviously have no ethics. But I want you to leave my aunt alone."

His face hardened. "How much do you really know about her?"

Misty gasped in outrage. "What are you implying? That Sophia would go along with you if she knew what you were up to?"

He looked perplexed. "I don't believe I understand."

"Don't play dumb with me! You and Warren expect to use her to finger your jobs—or whatever you criminals call it. But you won't get away with it. I'll go to the police if I have to!"

He stared at her in openmouthed amazement. "You think that I ... that we ..."

"That you're the cat burglars the police are looking for," she finished grimly.

Brandon started to laugh. "Dear little Misty. I do believe you've broken the world's record for jumping to wrong conclusions."

"I didn't expect you to admit it, but I'm warning you. I'll do exactly what I said if you try to involve Sophia."

His expression changed as he looked at her defiant face. "If you're so sure I'm a thief, why don't you go to the police anyway?"

Her eyes wavered. "I don't have any proof."

"You could tell them your suspicions. They'd watch me closely, maybe even run me out of town." When she didn't answer, he cupped her chin in his palm and forced her to look at him. "Wouldn't that be the sensible thing to do?"

"I don't want to hurt you, Brandon," she answered in a small voice. "I just have to protect Sophia."

"You're very sweet," he murmured huskily.

"Couldn't you get into another line of work?" she asked forlornly.

He folded her in his arms and kissed the top of her head. "I'm not a criminal, darling, in spite of what you think. I'll admit I lied to you, but not about anything that sinister."

Misty pulled out of his arms reluctantly. "I know what I heard, Brandon."

"But you misinterpreted it."

"Can you deny that you're working for Warren? Or that he said there was a lot of money involved?"

Brandon led her to a stone bench. "I see I'll have to tell you the whole story, but I must ask you not to tell anyone else, not even your aunt."

"I can't promise that."

"Perhaps you will after you hear what I have to say." He paused for a moment, choosing his words carefully. "To begin with, Warren was the friend I picked up at the airport. I brought him to Bootsy's party."

"I knew it!" Misty exclaimed. "I told Sophia you'd met before, but she didn't believe me."

An unreadable expression crossed his face. "I've underestimated you," he murmured.

"Why did you pretend to be strangers?"

"Warren is an old friend of my father's," he explained. "He asked my help in finding his youngest son, Robby. The kid has always been a problem. He grew up believing rules didn't apply to him, that his father's money gave him special privileges. When Warren finally refused to get him out of his latest jam, Robby ran away. He took some money and came to Europe, where he promptly got in with a bad crowd. Warren asked my help in tracking him down before the police do."

"You mean *he's* the cat burglar?"

"It's possible. Or he could be an accomplice of the person who is. Robby knows his way around café society, and he looks the part when he wears the right clothes."

"You've been looking for him in the jet-set hangouts?"

Brandon nodded. "Warren heard he was in Rome."

Misty tried to readjust her thinking. A great weight seemed to have lifted from her heart, but she had to be sure Brandon wasn't blowing smoke at her again.

"That still doesn't explain why you and Warren pretended not to know each other."

"If we both started asking questions, it would focus attention on the kid. We had to appear to meet accidentally so we wouldn't seem to have anything in common. Robby is a little jerk, but he's Warren's son. Warren doesn't want him to spend his life in prison. As you heard Warren point out, a lot of money is involved in these burglaries."

Misty thought back to the conversation she'd overheard. "He called you a professional. What did that mean?"

"A professional party-goer." Brandon smiled ruefully. "Warren needs my help, but I don't think he has a much higher opinion of me than he does of Robby."

It all fell into place except for one thing. "What does Sophia have to do with all this?"

"I couldn't keep taking Warren to the places where Robby might turn up, but Sophia could, so I steered him in her direction. Maybe it was a little devious, but that's all I did. If she hadn't liked him, she simply could have walked away."

"Was the rest of his story true? Is he really a widower?" Misty held her breath, waiting for the answer.

"That part's true," Brandon assured her.

She breathed a sigh of relief. "I'm so sorry, Brandon. But you can see how it sounded after everything that's happened." One last doubt surfaced. "You *were* the last person to dance with Bootsy before she discovered her ring was missing."

"If I'd wanted to steal it, I wouldn't have chosen someplace that public."

Misty realized the truth of his statement. He probably could have *talked* her out of it when they were alone!

"It's important that you don't repeat what I've just told you," Brandon said urgently. "If you tell Sophia and she tells just one person, and so on and so on, the story will be all over town. We'd never be able to get our hands on the kid."

Misty gave him a troubled look. "I can't let you take advantage of my aunt, even in a good cause. She likes Warren, and she thinks the feeling is reciprocated."

Brandon smiled a little wryly. "It is, honey. He feels badly about deceiving her. I've had a devil of a time convincing him it's necessary."

Misty brightened. "Sophia's awfully resourceful. Perhaps she could help."

"I have great admiration for your aunt's abilities," he answered a trifle grimly. "But I'd like to handle this myself. Warren's giving me enough problems. Would you just forget what you heard today?"

She remembered Brandon's remark that, if all went well, he might be going home. Was this his chance to prove to his father that he was capable of responsibility? Misty certainly didn't want to jeopardize the opportunity.

"You don't have to worry," she assured him. "I won't say a word."

He stared at her for a moment with an enigmatic expression. Brandon's face was almost hawklike, but his voice was gentle. "I wouldn't do it this way if it weren't vital."

"Just as long as Sophia doesn't get hurt."

"I don't want anyone to get hurt—especially you." He smoothed her hair tenderly.

She gazed up at him with relief. "I'm so glad everything is out in the open between us. I hated feeling I couldn't trust you."

Brandon uttered a sound that was almost a groan as he folded her in a smothering embrace. Her face was buried in his solid shoulder, and her breasts were crushed against his hard chest.

"Just remember that sometimes people have to do things they don't like very much," he said reluctantly.

She managed to draw back far enough to tilt her head up. "I understand that your first loyalty is to Warren. He's a friend, I'm just a . . . an acquaintance."

"You know better than that." The hard lines of his face softened as he stroked her cheek. "There's been magic between us from the beginning."

The proximity of his vibrant body was making Misty's legs tremble. Every taut muscle proclaimed Brandon's masculinity. She stared up at him with eyes like purple pansies, unable to deny the bond between them.

"You feel it, too, don't you, angel?"

"Yes," she whispered.

"My little love."

His kiss was slow and savoring at first, but it soon grew in intensity. His hands roamed over her back, urging her body against his taut frame, making her aware of his desire. Misty was drawn into a vortex of swirling emotion as Brandon's tongue parted her lips and probed with a symbolic male demand.

She was possessed by him, her defenses penetrated until she was a willing participant. Her fingers raked through his thick hair, and she pressed against him with a tiny sound of satisfaction. A mutual need gripped them both, blotting out any other consideration.

Brandon was the one who halted the escalation. He dragged his mouth away from hers and buried his face in her scented hair.

"If I don't stop, I'm going to take you right here on the grass," he said with a groan.

At that moment Misty would almost have agreed. She rested her cheek on his shoulder and waited for her heart to stop pounding. The distant sound of voices brought her back to reality.

She pulled out of Brandon's arms reluctantly. "We'd better go back," she murmured without looking directly at him.

"Unfortunately, you're right." His eyes were brilliant as he cupped her chin in his palm and gazed down at her. "Our time will come, though. You know that, don't you, sweetheart?"

Chapter Six

Sophia greeted Misty and Brandon with raised eyebrows when they returned to the table. "We were about to send out a scouting party," she remarked.

"Were we gone long?" Brandon asked innocently.

"Not in terms of space travel."

His eyes glinted mischievously. "The flowers were so fascinating, we couldn't tear ourselves away."

Sophia took note of her niece's flushed cheeks. "I thought it was something like that," she answered dryly.

"We're ready for our dessert now," Misty said hurriedly.

It was late afternoon by the time they finished lunch, but no one was in a hurry to start back.

"Let's walk down to the lake to see the swans before we leave," Misty suggested.

"Where are you getting all this energy, darling?" Sophia asked plaintively.

"From that tremendous lunch."

"She's right," Warren agreed. "I could do with a walk myself."

"I wish I'd saved a roll so I'd have something to feed the swans," Misty said.

"That's not an insurmountable problem." Brandon signaled the waiter.

When he explained what he wanted, the man returned with a paper bag full of dry bread. He also had a helpful suggestion. "Perhaps you would like to take the signorina for a canoe ride."

"What fun!" Misty exclaimed. "Could we, Brandon?"

"Are you going to paddle?" he teased.

"If necessary."

"It won't be." He put his arm around her shoulder and hugged her briefly. "You can lie back and trail your fingers in the water while I serenade you."

"I thought that's what one did in a gondola in Venice."

"Use your imagination," he advised.

"Come on, Sophia, Warren," Misty urged. "We'll have a race."

"How can I serenade you and compete at the same time?" Brandon complained.

"Can't you do two things at once?"

"Not and do justice to both."

He wasn't called upon to prove the point because the waiter said apologetically, "There is only one canoe."

"How sad," Sophia said with exaggerated regret.

"Yes, I was looking forward to working up a sweat in a leaky boat," Warren agreed dryly.

"You're older than I thought, Warren," Brandon said.

The other man laughed. "No, just wiser. You two run along and play in the water. Sophia and I will amuse ourselves in our own way."

"Okay, if that's the way you want it." Brandon took Misty's hand, and they walked down the sloping lawn to the lake.

The brightly painted canoe was tethered to a small tree at the water's edge. A pair of swans was floating nearby, but when Brandon helped Misty into the boat, the birds glided away.

"Hurry up," she urged as he untied the rope. "They're leaving."

"Toss them a piece of bread."

She reached into the bag and broke off a chunk of roll, but the swans kept going without a backward glance. "They didn't see it."

"Or maybe they don't like dry bread."

"Just my luck to run into a pair of gourmet birds," Misty grumbled.

Brandon finished coiling the rope in the bottom of the canoe and picked up a paddle. "Why don't you lie back and enjoy the scenery?" As the small boat slid noiselessly out toward the center of the lake he said, "Isn't it nifty?"

She gazed at the rolling hills covered with a low forest of grapevines that filled the air with a pungent aroma. Sunshine filtered through the dark, lacy leaves, forming a filigree pattern. Birds soared overhead in the blue sky, and butterflies fluttered like summer snowflakes among the trees that rimmed the lake.

"Is that the best you can do? Nifty?" she asked scornfully. "You have no romance in your soul."

"That's something I've never been accused of, but a canoe has limitations."

"Excuses, excuses."

"You're really asking for it, young lady. I'd make you change your tune if we were on solid ground."

"How?" she challenged, knowing he couldn't carry out his threat at the moment.

"I'd kiss you until your toes curled."

"That's not very romantic," she scoffed.

He grinned. "Don't knock it till you've tried it."

She wrinkled her nose. "You'll have to be more persuasive than that."

"Okay, how's this?" Brandon's voice dropped a couple of notches until it was as warm and liquid as the water around them. "If we were alone under those trees, I'd make love to you very slowly. First I'd kiss your eyelids and each corner of your lovely mouth. Then I'd touch that enchanting little hollow in your throat with the tip of my tongue."

"I get the picture," Misty said hastily.

"Quiet, woman, you asked for this." His voice was a velvet purr as he murmured, "I'd lie beside you on the grass and cover your beautiful body with kisses until I found the spot that gave you the most pleasure."

"Brandon, this has really gone far enough!"

His eyes glittered as he continued inexorably. "I'd caress every exquisite inch of you, until you held out your arms and called my name."

His arousing words were making her heart pound. Misty knew she would react in just that manner if they were ever in the situation he was describing. She could almost feel his fingertips feathering over her body in an erotic pattern, his mouth fanning embers into flames.

"Please, Brandon." She moistened her lips nervously and dropped her eyes to the roll in her clenched hands. When he ignored her whispered words, continuing his seduction, she broke off little pieces of bread and threw them into the water.

"Yes, darling, I'll please you, I promise," he said huskily. "It's going to be so good with us."

What happened next was so swift and unexpected that they were both taken by surprise. Misty was completely tangled in Brandon's spell, unaware of the swans' approach. They had followed the trail of bread chunks to the canoe, gobbling up each one.

When they reached the boat, both birds uttered a raucous cry and bent their long necks toward the remaining bread in Misty's hands. She jerked back instinctively and half rose from the seat, startled by their long beaks.

"Don't stand up!" Brandon shouted.

His warning came too late. Her sharp movement had rocked the unstable boat. It turned over, dumping them both in the water.

Everything was a blur after that. Misty had a moment of terror as she was trapped under the canoe. Her head had bobbed to the surface, but she felt as though she were suffocating in the darkness. Then Brandon grabbed her and pulled her out from under the boat.

"Are you all right?" His face was concerned as he supported her weight.

She clasped her arms around his neck, gasping and sputtering. "I guess so. What happened?"

The strain on his face was replaced by a smile as he gently brushed the wet hair out of her eyes. "You got your wish to feed the swans."

"They picked a fine time to change their eating habits." She looked at the silk shirt collar plastered to his neck. "Oh, Brandon, your clothes are ruined. I'm so sorry."

"Don't worry about it," he said as Sophia and Warren called out anxiously from shore. "Can you tread water while I right the canoe?"

"We'll never get back into that thing. Let's swim."

"Good idea."

Sophia and Warren were waiting for them when they waded ashore, their clothes stuck to their bodies.

"What on earth happened out there?" Sophia exclaimed.

Brandon grinned. "Misty learned the hard way that you can't stand up in a canoe."

"You're both going to catch cold if you don't get out of those soaked things," Sophia fussed.

The breeze that had been so balmy was now chilling against their wet skin. Misty shivered, pulling her sodden clothing away from her clammy body.

"We don't have anything to change into," she pointed out.

"Well, you can't go home dripping like that," Sophia said. "You'll catch pneumonia."

Warren had a suggestion. "I'm sure the inn has an empty room. While they get warmed up, we'll drive back to the hotel for dry clothes."

"That's an excellent idea," Sophia said.

Misty wasn't so sure. "Maybe they could just give us some towels to dry off."

"Nonsense! Your teeth are chattering already," her aunt said. "By the time we drove all the way back to Rome, you'd be a block of ice."

"Sophia's right." Brandon was struggling to contain his amusement. He knew why Misty wasn't enthusiastic about the plan. "I don't fancy that long ride in this condition."

"It's out of the question," Sophia declared. "Come along, you both need to take a hot shower immediately."

She took over, and there wasn't anything Misty could do about it. No other alternative presented itself. A room was secured at the inn, and Sophia told them to order hot coffee and a bottle of brandy.

"We'll be back as soon as possible," she promised.

Brandon grinned impudently. "Take your time."

The small room seemed very intimate after the other two had left. Outside of one straight chair and a dresser, it was dominated by a bed covered with a puffy quilt.

Misty cleared her throat. "Shall we toss to see who gets the first shower?"

Brandon had removed his jacket and was unbuttoning his shirt. "You take it. Just give me one of those robes, and I'll get undressed while you're in there."

She bolted into the bathroom and grabbed one of the thick terry-cloth robes provided by most European hotels.

Brandon was shrugging off his shirt when she returned. The broad expanse of his chest was tautly muscled and very tan. After a swift glance, Misty averted her eyes and handed him the robe.

Instead of taking it, his fingers curled around her wrist. "Relax, honey. I'm not going to pounce on you."

"I know that," she mumbled.

"Then why are you so nervous?"

"You have to admit this is a rather unconventional situation."

He chuckled. "Only if we showered together. Which is a splendid idea, incidentally."

"That's what you had in mind all along," she accused. "Admit it!"

"I wasn't the one who turned over the canoe," he answered mildly.

She gasped. "You think I did that on purpose?"

"It was a rather drastic move, and totally unnecessary. You could have had me just by asking." His eyes twinkled.

Misty knew he was teasing her and enjoying her reaction. The women he was accustomed to didn't blush and stammer in the bedroom. She couldn't do anything about her high color, but she could at least match his joking tone.

"I'd take you up on your proposition if I weren't so cold," she said lightly.

"Would you really?" The hand he hooked around her neck prevented her from moving away.

When his fingers started to massage the sensitive spot at her nape, Misty's composure fled. "No, of course not!" She started to tremble, every nerve in her body responding to his masculinity.

Brandon's teasing manner vanished. "You really are cold, aren't you? You're shivering. Get into a hot shower, honey."

"Yes, I . . . I think I'd better."

Misty closed her eyes and let the warm water flow over her body, willing herself to relax. Brandon wasn't going to make a pass at her unless she invited one, so it was pointless—not to mention humiliating—to behave like a shy schoolgirl. Why couldn't she act naturally around him? With any other man this would be a hilarious incident. Why did the thought of going back into the bedroom with nothing on under a robe tie her in knots? The thought of Brandon similarly attired sent her blood pressure soaring.

Misty resolutely closed her mind to the vision. Sophia and Warren would be back as soon as possible, and this whole ordeal would be over. She groaned softly, knowing how the minutes were going to drag.

"Are you all right?" Brandon called through the door.

"Yes, I'm fine," she called back hastily. "I'll be out in a minute."

"No hurry. I just got worried because you were so quiet in there."

The soap dish clattered to the floor as Misty grabbed a washcloth and quickly lathered her body. She finished by rinsing the pond water out of her hair.

After twisting a towel around her head like a turban, she dried herself vigorously with another towel. By the time she slipped into the long white terry-cloth robe, her skin was glowing like a ripe peach.

She tightened the belt around her slender waist as she went into the bedroom. "Okay, it's all yours."

"Are you warmer now?" Brandon asked with lingering concern.

"Back to normal," she assured him.

"You certainly don't look any the worse for wear." His eyes admired her exquisite coloring.

"Except that my hair is a mess and all my makeup washed off," she said ruefully.

"I like you this way." His voice deepened. "You look as though you just got out of bed."

She turned away abruptly. "You'd better take your shower. Sophia and Warren will be back soon."

"We have plenty of time for the important things," he answered softly.

Misty turned indignantly, but Brandon had vanished into the bathroom, leaving his words to linger in the air like a promise. A moment later she heard him singing as he turned on the water.

Brandon didn't linger in the shower as she had. He was in and out in a very short time. Misty was combing her damp hair when he returned to the bedroom wearing a robe that matched hers. The difference was that hers reached to the floor while Brandon's only skimmed his calves. He didn't have to turn the sleeves up, either.

"That's what I need," he said, running his fingers through his thick hair.

"You can use mine if you like," Misty offered.

"I didn't like to ask. Some people consider a comb as personal as a toothbrush."

She smiled. "I wouldn't offer to let you use my toothbrush."

He crossed the room to stand over her. "That's all right. I'll take whatever you're willing to give me."

As their eyes met in the mirror, she held up the comb.

Brandon chuckled. "That's the extent of it? Okay, my elusive maiden, but someday you might have regrets."

"Let me worry about that," she said tartly.

"Virtue is its own reward?" He laughed.

Misty twisted around to look up at him. "Why is *virtue* such a dirty word?" she flared. "It's better than falling in and out of bed with strangers."

His eyes narrowed. "Is that what you think I do?"

"It's none of my business," she muttered.

"That means you do."

"Well, maybe not strangers, but you have an awful lot of close friends."

"You know that for a fact?" he asked coolly.

"I've seen you operate. I'm not a child," she snapped.

"Sometimes you act remarkably like one."

Misty stood up, drawing herself to her full height. "I'm sorry that I'm not as sophisticated as your blond girlfriend."

A slight frown creased Brandon's forehead as he stared down at her. "I don't know what this fixation is you have over Bootsy."

"I don't happen to find her as charming as you do."

"That isn't a word that applies to her. She's spoiled rotten, and her manners are atrocious."

"Then how can you—" Misty stopped abruptly.

"How can I what? Make love to her? That's what you want to know, isn't it?"

"No! I mean, it doesn't matter to me!" She snatched the comb back and started raking it through her hair.

"But you wonder what I see in her." He watched her with a mocking smile. "Surely you can't be that naïve. A man like me wants only one thing from a woman. Isn't that right?" When Misty didn't answer, he whirled her around to face him, his hands biting into her shoulders. "Answer me!"

"What do you want me to say?" Her eyes were a deep purple in their frame of sooty lashes. "You've admitted you don't even like Bootsy, yet there's obviously some relationship between you. It doesn't take a genius to figure out what kind."

"It never occurred to you to give me the benefit of a doubt, I suppose," he said bitingly.

Misty's misery was reflected on her face, yet she couldn't back down. "I don't *have* any doubt."

Brandon's hands tightened as he gave her a little shake. "Even though I've told you about Warren's son?"

"Is Bootsy the only person who can help you?" she countered.

"She's the most abundant source of information. Bootsy is the clearinghouse for gossip in Rome. She knows who's arriving, when they're leaving, what parties are scheduled—even what outfit and jewelry the women are going to wear."

Misty's lip curled. "Minding everyone's business must keep her hopping."

He shrugged. "It's a way of life for these people."

She was reminded that he was one of "these people." "How do you stand it, Brandon?" she burst out.

"It's getting harder every day," he admitted grimly.

"Then why don't you get out? Go home and *do* something with your life!"

He hesitated. "There's no point in asking you to trust me, because you obviously don't. Just try to keep an open mind," he pleaded.

"About Bootsy, you mean?"

"About everything." He raised her chin and gazed deeply into her eyes. "You and I have something very special going for us. I felt it from the beginning, and I think you did, too."

Misty steeled herself against his potent magnetism. Brandon could charm a mummy out of her wrappings. He'd perfected that urgent tone of voice, that devouring gaze that made a woman feel she was the only one who mattered to him. His caressing hands and potent masculinity were added weapons in an impressive arsenal.

"What we felt was physical attraction," she said flatly. "That isn't even very special. You seem to feel the same way toward a lot of women."

"How about you, Misty?" he asked softly. "Do you melt in other men's arms the way you do in mine?"

"I don't think that's any of your business," she answered stiffly.

"You're wrong, my little love. I'm trying to make you admit there's more than sex between us."

"Can you deny you've been trying to get me into bed ever since we met?" she demanded.

"I want to make love to you—there's a difference."

"Oh, please, Brandon!"

He combed his fingers through the soft cloud of her hair, drawing it back from her face so he could scan each delicately chiseled feature. "Of course I want to possess you. What man wouldn't? You're like an exquisite porcelain figurine, but under that cool surface are banked fires. I want to hold you in my arms and let the fire weld us together."

A quiver ran through her at the thought of Brandon's lean body poised over hers, his thrusting masculinity filling her with ecstasy. She forced the erotic picture from her mind.

"It won't work, Brandon," she said grimly. "For once in your life, you're going to strike out."

"You don't intend to see me again?"

She bit her lip, unwilling to make the break final. "That's not . . . I mean, I don't imagine you want to see *me* again, under the circumstances."

"I can't think of any circumstance when I wouldn't want to see you." He stroked her cheek tenderly. "You're the one bright spot in my day. I look forward to being with you and begrudge the time when I can't."

The tight knot in Misty's chest dissolved. "You want to go on the way we were in spite of . . . well, everything?"

His green eyes danced with mischief. "On one condition."

"What's that?" she asked warily.

"That I get to kiss you on special occasions."

"Like what?"

"Mondays if the museums are closed, Tuesdays if it doesn't rain."

Sheer joy coursed through Misty. She tipped her head, appearing to consider. "That sounds fair. How about the rest of the week?"

"A holiday is bound to turn up. Every day is cause for celebration when I'm with you," he said huskily.

"Do you really mean that, Brandon?" she asked searchingly. "You're not just expecting me to change my mind?"

"I hope you do, sweetheart, because I want you more than I've ever wanted any woman. But that's not all I feel for you. I love your loyalty and lack of pretension. I enjoy your fresh delight in everything around you, and your quick mind and your laughter." His eyes held tenderness rather than passion. "I like you."

"Oh, Brandon, that's lovely." Impulsively, Misty put her arms around his waist and rested her head on his chest.

He held her and stroked her hair gently. "Will you try to trust me from now on?"

She sighed. "I didn't mean to sound like an outraged virgin. I'm not like that normally."

He chuckled and kissed the top of her head. "I know, darling. Your response has been very satisfactory for the most part."

She tilted her head to look up at him. "I *am* attracted to you, Brandon. I won't try to deny it. But the thought of being part of a passing parade just isn't my style."

"It isn't mine either, honey. I won't try to pretend I've led a monastic life. I'm a man, not a boy. But I've had relationships, not indiscriminate sex."

"We wouldn't have had time for a relationship anyway," she said in a small voice.

"Don't you believe it," he answered deeply.

"Two weeks is just . . . an interlude."

"Who set that time limit?"

"I guess Sophia will want to leave after the big party," Misty said forlornly. "We'll probably never see each other again."

"How could you think a thing like that?" He gazed at her lovingly. "You can't get rid of me that easily."

"I don't really want to," she murmured.

He gave her a hug. "Sweet little Misty."

She looked up at him through long lashes. "This is shaping up as a special occasion, wouldn't you say?"

Sudden awareness smoldered in his eyes. "A very definite occasion."

He lowered his head so he could claim her lips. Excitement raced through Misty's veins as Brandon's mouth moved over hers, savoring the yielding softness. Any remaining reservations were buried under an avalanche of sensation. She clasped her arms around his neck and pressed close to his hard frame.

His arms tightened at her response, and he parted her lips with his tongue, probing the moist recess with an expertise that made her legs feel weak. When she clung to him for support, Brandon buried his face in the damp softness of her hair.

"My dear little love," he murmured. "You're so warm, so giving."

"Never like this before." She stirred restlessly in his arms. "I'm a different person with you. I can't explain it."

"Don't question magic, sweetheart."

"Maybe that's what it is. Sometimes I think you've cast a spell over me."

He smiled at her sober face. "Then the tables were turned. I'm the one who's bewitched."

In spite of his words, Misty knew, Brandon was in complete command of himself—as he would always be. His emotions would never rule him. He would always know exactly what he was doing.

"You could be a very dangerous man," she whispered.

His smile fled. "I'd never hurt you, my love."

Misty knew he could hurt her a great deal. He might very easily break her heart. Yet suddenly, it didn't matter. She'd played it safe all her life, but no more. This man was everything she'd always dreamed of. He could bring her untold bliss. And if heaven came with a price tag, well, so be it.

She stood on tiptoe and reached for Brandon's lips. When his mouth closed over hers, she was the one who deepened the kiss. He made a little sound of pleasure, but when she pushed his robe open so she could caress his bare chest, he stiffened.

As she ran her palms over his flat nipples, he groaned. Misty continued her exploration of his body, raking her nails lightly through the dark mat of hair that cushioned the hard wall of his chest, then trailing her fingers down to his stomach. The rigid muscles tightened even more when she reached his navel and circled the small depression.

Brandon's hand closed over hers like a vise. "You're playing with fire, little one," he warned.

She laughed softly. "You do seem rather warm."

His eyes narrowed. "I never figured you for a tease."

She put her arms around his neck and tilted her head to gaze up at him. "For an experienced man, you're awfully dense."

He scanned her dreamy face with dawning excitement. "You mean—"

"Do I have to ask you to make love to me?"

Brandon's arms were like steel bands as he strained her against him convulsively. "I want you so much! Tell me I'm not dreaming."

Misty's kiss did more than that. It conveyed the deep longing that matched his. They were both taut with desire, trembling with their need for each other.

His hands roamed restlessly over her back, urging her body closer as he muttered incoherent words interspersed with burning kisses over her face and neck. The force of his passion swept away all of Misty's inhibitions. She ached to feel the piercing wonder of this man. But when she reached down to untie his belt, a tremor ran through him, and he caught her hand. His breathing was ragged as he put her gently away.

Misty couldn't comprehend his actions. Her face was bewildered as she stared up at him. "Brandon?" she whispered uncertainly.

"I can't do it." His voice was uneven with the effort it took.

Tears clogged her throat suddenly. "You don't want me? It was all a big joke?"

"If you only knew how much I want you!" He folded her in his arms once more and gently cradled her head on his shoulder. "I'd like to carry you over to that bed and keep you there for a week. I want to make love to you every way there is, and then make up new ways to bring you pleasure."

"Then why—"

"Because you're too sweet and trusting. I'd be taking advantage of your generosity, and you might hate me afterward."

"I could never hate you, Brandon. I—" Misty stopped as a thunderous revelation struck. She loved him! It wasn't just the awesome physical attraction between them. What she felt was true, everlasting love!

He massaged the taut muscles in his neck distractedly. "This situation we're in is very provocative."

Her newfound knowledge filled Misty with tenderness. Brandon was obviously suffering. "You mean because we're alone in a hotel room with nothing on but bathrobes?" she murmured.

"Yes," he replied curtly.

"Then maybe we should take them off." She slowly untied her belt and let the robe slide off her shoulders.

"Don't do this to me," he begged hoarsely, his eyes devouring her body. "I'm trying to restrain myself."

"I'd rather you didn't," she answered demurely.

Brandon's resistance collapsed, and he reached out to touch her, almost reverently. "I've dreamed about this moment, but you're even more exquisite than I could have imagined."

His fingertips feathered over her breasts, creating a pulsing excitement deep in her midsection. Misty closed her eyes as his hands moved over her body in a slow exploration that was almost unbearably erotic. The sensual caresses promised ultimate fulfillment, tantalizing her at the prospect. She uttered a tiny sound that was part pleasure, part plea.

Brandon dipped his head and kissed one taut nipple. "You do want me, don't you, sweetheart?" he murmured.

"So much," she breathed, clutching his shoulders for support.

"I want it to be as special for you as it is for me," he said huskily.

Lifting her in his arms, he carried her to the bed, where he stretched out beside her to continue his slow devastation. Misty quivered when his lips trailed over her body, leaving excitement in their wake. She twisted restlessly as his hands stroked the smooth plane of her stomach, and drew a sharp breath when he reached the juncture of her thighs. As his caresses became more intimate she arched her body.

"You're driving me wild," she gasped.

Brandon's eyes glittered as he stared at the abandoned passion on her face. "Tell me what you want, my love. I need to hear you say it."

She reached for him blindly, hungering for his hard body. Only this man could fill the aching void that was both a torment and a joy.

As she parted her lips to whisper the words that would open the gates of paradise, she felt him stiffen and raise his head. It was only then that Misty heard the voices in the hallway. They were followed by a knock on the door.

"We're back," Sophia called gaily.

Brandon swore savagely under his breath as he quickly helped Misty to a sitting position. When she stared at him in a daze he said in a low voice, "Go into the bathroom. I'll tell them you're combing your hair."

She let him lead her like a child, too bemused to take any action herself.

He draped her robe around her shoulders and held her close for a long moment. Then he kissed her gently. "This is just an intermission, sweetheart," he said tenderly.

He urged her into the bathroom and closed the door. Tightening the belt on his bathrobe, Brandon went to greet the others.

"When you didn't answer the door, I thought for a minute I had the wrong room," Sophia said.

"Were you out there long?" Brandon asked innocently. "I must have dozed off."

"Where's Misty?" she asked.

"I guess she's still in the bathroom, fixing her face or something."

"We got back as fast as we could."

"You really didn't have to hurry. We were doing fine." Brandon's grim expression didn't match his reassuring words.

"Did you both take a hot shower?" she persisted.

"I could do with a cold one," he muttered under his breath.

"What?" She looked at him sharply.

After a glance at Brandon's set face, Warren provided a distraction. "Misty must be waiting for her things," he reminded her.

"You're right." She went to the bathroom door and knocked. "It's Sophia, darling. I have dry clothes for you."

Misty hadn't recovered her equilibrium as fast as Brandon. She had sunk slowly onto the edge of the bathtub, waiting for the hot tide of desire to ebb. Every fiber of her body still vibrated from his touch. How could she join the others and act as though nothing had happened? Her whole life had been turned around by the realization of her love for Brandon. It couldn't help but show on her face, but no one must know until she found out if he felt the same way. Sophia's knock brought Misty reluctantly to her feet.

"I brought slacks and a sweater because I figured there was no point in getting dressed up again," Sophia said, holding out a pair of beige silk pants and a matching blouse. "You'll want to change for dinner, anyway."

"These are fine," Misty said vaguely.

Sophia stared at her with a slight frown. "Are you all right? You look strange."

Misty managed a laugh. "An unexpected dunking does nothing for one's hairdo."

"It isn't that. Your cheeks are flushed, and your eyes are too bright. I knew it! You've caught cold."

"That's ridiculous. I'm perfectly all right."

Sophia put the back of her hand on Misty's flushed cheek. "No, you're not. You have a fever."

"What's all the fuss?" Brandon came to the door. He was now wearing light gray slacks with a white silk shirt and a navy sweater.

"Misty's coming down with something," Sophia announced. "Look at her face."

"It looks beautiful to me," Brandon said softly.

"This is no time to be gallant," Sophia answered impatiently. "Can't you see how flushed she is? I wish I'd brought some aspirin."

Warren's impassive eyes intercepted the glance between Brandon and Misty. "I'm sure it's nothing serious," he said dryly.

"Of course not." Misty snatched the clothes out of Sophia's hands. "If you'll give me a minute to get dressed, we can get out of here." Pushing her aunt out of the bathroom, she shut the door and pulled on her clothes swiftly.

Misty tried to hide her tension, but she was wound as tightly as a steel coil, and Sophia sensed it. The older woman fussed over her from a deep feeling of affection.

In the car going back to Rome she said, "You're going straight to bed when we get to the hotel. And if you're not better in the morning, I'm calling the doctor."

"That's the silliest notion I ever heard of!" Misty exclaimed. "There's not a thing on earth wrong with me."

"I hope not. But who knows what kind of germs were in that pond? I won't let your vacation be spoiled by a silly mishap," Sophia stated firmly.

Misty looked helplessly at Brandon. She had counted on spending the evening with him. So many things needed to be said between them. But her aunt could be surprisingly adamant when she considered it important.

Brandon squeezed her hand on the seat between them. "I'm very good at waiting," he said softly.

Misty wished she had his fortitude. A tiny chill touched her spine. Did that mean she wasn't that important to him? She stole a look at his strong profile as he watched the road.

Brandon was in complete command of himself, as always. She might almost have imagined the importunate lover who had shuddered with desire against her. Did the act of love involve any deeper feelings for him? Or was his passion easily aroused and just as easily suppressed because it was merely sexual?

Misty was very quiet on the drive back.

Chapter Seven

Sophia ordered dinner in their suite that night, ignoring Misty's plea that she keep her date with Warren.

"I won't sneak out," she promised.

"I know that, but I want to be here, darling. I was terribly worried when I saw that canoe go over."

"I don't know why. I can swim."

"You might have banged your head when you went under. Dear Warren was preparing to swim out and rescue you."

Misty looked obliquely at her aunt. Sophia's face had a soft glow. "Was he upset that I ruined his day?" she asked.

"You didn't at all. We had a lovely lunch."

"But then you had that long trip to Rome and back."

Sophia smiled. "It wasn't a hardship."

"What did you talk about all that time?" Misty asked casually.

"Oh, this and that."

"Nothing special, in other words."

Sophia gazed at her with raised eyebrows. "You were never any good at subterfuge, pet. What are you getting at?"

"Nothing! I was just . . . making conversation."

"Since when do you and I have to look for things to talk about?"

"We don't, of course. I just wondered how things were progressing with you and Warren," Misty explained carefully. "You expressed a lot of interest in him today."

Her aunt was distracted, as Misty had meant her to be. "I haven't felt this way about a man since Lucien died," she admitted. "In fact, I never expected to again."

Misty's heart sank. In spite of Brandon's assurances, she still had a lot of qualms. "You haven't known him very long," she remarked tentatively.

"If you'd ever been in love, you'd know it isn't a matter of time."

Misty was shocked. "You're in love with him?"

Sophia hesitated. "I could be."

"But you don't know anything about him!"

"I know he's kind and thoughtful—besides being the most stimulating man I've met in ages. I can talk to Warren. He's intelligent, and he has a sense of humor."

"Those are the qualities you look for in a friend," Misty protested.

Sophia laughed softly. "I'm also attracted to him in other ways. I just didn't think it was something an aunt told her niece."

Misty smiled reluctantly. "I can discuss the birds and bees without blushing."

"I'm glad to hear it, darling. I was afraid your mother's primness had rubbed off on you."

Misty thought about the interlude in Brandon's arms. Her whole body heated in remembrance. Sophia wouldn't be shocked, but it wasn't something she was ready to share.

"We were talking about you and Warren," she said. "He's very nice, but don't you think you ought to go slowly?"

Sophia sighed. "Just when I was beginning to have hopes for you. I can hear my sister's words coming out of your mouth."

"What's wrong with being a little cautious?" Misty asked defensively. "That's all I'm suggesting."

"Play it safe? Don't get involved? If I'd lived my life that way, I'd never have met Lucien."

"But all men aren't like him," Misty said urgently. "The fact that you lucked out once doesn't mean lightning will strike twice."

"I have the feeling you're trying to tell me something," Sophia said slowly. "Do you know something about Warren that I don't?"

Misty's promise to Brandon wouldn't have deterred her if she'd thought Sophia's happiness was in jeopardy. But suppose he was telling the truth? Did she have the right to raise doubts in Sophia's mind, perhaps cause a rift between her and Warren because of a vague uneasiness? Maybe she was letting her own insecurity with Brandon color her thinking. Misty knew she'd never forgive herself if she destroyed a meaningful relationship for her aunt out of misguided concern. Better by far to wait and watch.

"I only know what he told us," she said carefully. "I merely wondered if he told you any more. Perhaps some details of his family life."

"We don't discuss our previous spouses, if that's what you mean."

"How about children? Did Warren say anything about them?"

"No, I gather they're grown and leading their own lives. It's rather sad that he didn't have any girls. They usually remain closer to their parents."

"I'm surprised he'd take a trip like this all alone."

"I consider it admirable. The alternative is staying home and vegetating."

"Not exactly. He must meet a lot of high-powered people in the oil business. Has he mentioned any of them?"

Sophia sighed again. "You're convinced he's a phony, aren't you?"

"No, I . . . I just want to be sure he isn't using you."

Her aunt looked amused. "If he's interested in my money, we're both in for a rude awakening."

"I wasn't suggesting that. I merely wondered . . ." Misty paused, choosing her words carefully. "You can open a lot of doors for him."

"You think Warren is a social climber?"

"I don't know *what* he is. Just be careful, Sophia! I don't want you to get hurt."

"Life doesn't offer that guarantee," her aunt said gently. "Nor does it give unlimited chances. You reach for happiness when it comes within your grasp."

"Even if it's only temporary?"

"How would you know if you held back?"

"It might be easier to give up something you never had," Misty said somberly, no longer thinking only of her aunt's problem.

Sophia looked at her shrewdly. "If a woman gives up a man she truly loves, she's either a coward or a fool. Neither you nor I fit that description."

Sophia didn't, anyway. "I wish I could be more like you," Misty said impulsively.

The older woman smiled fondly at her. "You are, darling. You just don't realize it."

Misty slept late the next morning after the traumatic events of the day before. She awoke refreshed and eager for the day ahead.

The talk with her aunt had clarified things in her mind. Life had presented her with a priceless gift. Only an idiot would refuse it.

Sophia was already dressed when Misty went into the living room in her bathrobe. She was sitting at the ornate French desk going over some correspondence.

"Good morning, pet." The other woman looked up in greeting. "How do you feel this morning?"

Misty stretched her arms wide. "I feel wonderful!"

"You look a lot better, too—not so tense. A good night's sleep was what you needed."

"I suppose so. Were there any calls?" Misty asked casually.

"An endless amount."

"For me, I mean."

Sophia glanced down at a slip of paper. "Duane Creighton phoned twice. He said he'd call back. A young man named Baldwin just called five minutes ago and left an urgent message for you to please return his call." She looked up through half glasses. "You made quite a hit at Bootsy's party."

Misty couldn't have cared less. They weren't the ones she wanted to hear from. Her happiness diminished slightly. She'd thought Brandon would phone bright and early.

"Are those all the calls there were for me?"

"The line's been busy," Sophia said gently. "Brandon might have had trouble getting through."

How hard had he tried? Misty attempted to look uninterested. "What makes you think I was asking about *him*?"

Sophia wasn't put off by her distant tone. "He'll get in touch with you, don't worry."

Misty gave up the pretense. "I wish I had your confidence." She sighed. "When we're together I get the feeling that he...he enjoys my company. But then I never hear from him again."

Sophia glanced at her watch. "It's only eleven in the morning. Don't you think you're jumping to conclusions? Even supermen sleep late sometimes."

Misty eagerly grabbed the reassurance she was looking for. Her aunt had given two reasons why Brandon hadn't phoned yet. But he would. After yesterday he surely would! Her faith was justified when the telephone rang.

"Yes, she's awake," Sophia said. She held out the receiver. "It's Duane."

Misty's expectant expression dimmed as she took the phone. "Hi, Duane," she said neutrally.

"Light of my life, where have you been? I've been trying to get in touch with you for days!"

"I've been out a lot."

"Were you being untrue to me with the Roman legions?" he demanded.

"No, only one man."

"Tell me the blackguard's name, and I'll do bodily harm to the rascal."

Misty smiled. "I believe he goes by the name of Conan the Barbarian."

"Oh. Well, in that case perhaps I'll just tie his shoelaces together. Tell him he's in for a nasty fall."

"I'll deliver the message," she promised.

"Let's work on the wording tonight over dinner."

"Not tonight, Duane."

"You're seeing muscle man again?"

"I . . . I'm busy this evening."

"How about tomorrow night? I'm not going to give up," he warned.

"My plans are a little indefinite," she hedged. "Why don't you call me?" After much evasion, Misty eased him off the phone.

"You didn't mention having a date this evening," Sophia commented when Misty had hung up.

"Duane's rather lightweight," she answered vaguely.

"Still, a little competition is sometimes a good thing. It makes a man appreciate you."

Misty's lip curled with distaste. "I don't play games."

"You just played one with Duane by implying you had a date tonight."

"I didn't feel like seeing him," Misty answered defensively.

"Why didn't you say so?"

"You don't go out of your way to hurt someone's feelings," Misty protested.

"What are you going to do when he calls again?"

"I don't know." Misty looked doubtfully at her aunt. "Do you *want* me to go out with Duane?"

"That's for you to decide. I just don't want you to waste your time hanging around the suite."

"You don't think Brandon's going to call, do you?" Misty asked soberly.

"Stop putting words in my mouth and go get dressed." Sophia's brisk tone masked her sympathy.

Misty's thoughts were somber as she soaked in a bubble bath. For all of Sophia's reassurances, her aunt didn't put a lot of faith in Brandon's dependability, either. But she didn't know what had taken place at the inn.

Misty's eyes grew dreamy as she remembered that stirring hour, reliving every sensual caress, every husky word Brandon had murmured. "This is just an intermission," he'd said. When she recalled the tenderness in his voice, the warmth of his embrace, how could she doubt him?

Sophia was ready to go out when Misty rejoined her in the living room after getting dressed.

"Would you like to have lunch?" Sophia asked. "I'm meeting some friends from London. I think you'd enjoy them."

"I'm sure I would, but no thanks. Go ahead and have fun."

"What are you going to do?"

"I haven't seen half of Rome yet," Misty answered evasively.

Sophia paused indecisively. "You have to eat. Why not join us? You can go exploring afterward."

"I know how long your lunches last. Go on or you'll be late."

"Well, if you're sure." Her aunt gave in reluctantly.

The phone rang frequently after she left, but the calls were all for Sophia. As the clock ticked off the minutes,

Misty's heart grew heavier and heavier. Finally at two o'clock she faced the fact that Brandon wasn't going to call.

It seemed utterly incomprehensible. She hadn't imagined his passion in that hotel room. He had wanted her as much as she wanted him. Then *why*?

It was just one more puzzling aspect of a man who was a total enigma. Had his response been just male reaction to a female body? Was he keeping her dangling for reasons of his own?

All of Misty's suspicions returned in full force. Brandon's deception about knowing Warren, his story about Robby—that might or might not be true—his urgent plea that she keep his secret from Sophia. Who was Brandon Powers really, and what game was he playing?

When she couldn't stand her own thoughts anymore, Misty grabbed her purse and left the suite.

She walked the short distance to the Spanish Steps and stood at the top, gazing down at the broad expanse dotted with tourists. Some were taking pictures of the magnificent twin-towered church, Trinità dei Monti, which crowned the summit. Others were gaping at the orange trees and the stately palms that seemed so out of place in this climate.

She threaded her way through the sightseers to the even more crowded sidewalk below. Street artists were urging watercolor scenes of Rome on passersby, while vendors hawked cheap souvenirs. The carnival atmosphere was noisy and colorful.

Misty skirted the flower carts displaying feathery bouquets of yellow mimosa and wandered aimlessly until she reached the Via Condotti. The multitude of shops with their variety of merchandise distracted her, and she forgot her problems temporarily.

The windows were full of tempting items—clothing, leather goods, china—all beautiful and costly. She couldn't resist going inside to browse, even though she had no intention of buying anything. The prices were astronomical, even when translated from lire into American money.

When her feet started to ache from the uneven pavement, she stopped at a small café and ordered a cappuccino. As she sipped the foamy concoction she couldn't help remembering that the last time she'd sat at a sidewalk café had been with Brandon.

How had he spent the day? And with whom? Misty tried to concentrate on the throngs of people passing by, but it was no use. Every tall, broad-shouldered man reminded her of him. Finally she put some coins on the table and left.

Dusk was softening the contours of the city when she returned to the hotel. The view from their hotel suite was an indistinct blur of spires and arches silhouetted against the darkening sky.

Sophia greeted her from the couch where she was reading a newspaper. "Hello, darling. Did you have a nice day? Sit down and bring me up-to-date on the latest in antiquities."

Misty kicked off her shoes and sank gratefully into a chair. "They're a lot more durable than I am."

"Culture takes its toll." Sophia smiled. "What wonders of the ancient world did you see today?"

"The Spanish Steps and the Trinità dei Monti, although I didn't go inside."

"You really must before we leave. It's quite impressive. What else did you do? That couldn't have taken all afternoon."

"I went shopping on the Via Condotti. They have beautiful things, but what prices!"

"Yes, it's not for bargain hunters."

"I was almost tempted to buy something just so I could say it cost a hundred thousand lire. That sounds so impressive."

"At those prices you feel like leaving the tag attached," Sophia agreed. "Where did you have lunch?"

Misty was reminded that she hadn't eaten all day. She knew her aunt would be concerned, so she said, "Rome is full of sidewalk cafés." That wasn't a lie.

"Aren't they charming? Did any of those gorgeous Italian men try to pick you up?"

"No."

"That's rather unbelievable." Sophia gazed at her niece's lovely face and slender figure. "You're too unapproachable, that's your problem."

"At least I'm doing one thing right," Misty replied grimly. "Evidently no one ever told you that you can get in a lot of trouble picking up strange men." That's how the whole thing with Brandon had started.

"I was only suggesting a pleasant conversation over a cup of espresso. It's fun to get to know the natives."

"I didn't feel like talking to anyone," Misty answered curtly.

Sophia slanted a glance at her shadowed eyes. "You look frazzled, pet. Why don't you take a little nap before dinner?"

"Maybe I will." Misty stood up and managed a smile for her aunt. "Sight-seeing is hard work."

"You'll bounce back. Warren is taking us to a new disco tonight."

Misty paused on her way to the bedroom. "Count me out."

"I'll do nothing of the sort."

"He asked you, not me. I'm not intruding on your date."

"That's a silly way to look at it. Warren will be delighted."

"I'm sure that's just what he had in mind—a candlelight supper for three."

"Why don't we discuss it when you're more rested?"

"There is nothing to discuss," Misty said firmly.

After taking off her clothes she curled up under the bed's down duvet. Sophia meant well, but Misty had no intention of being a fifth wheel—tonight, or any subsequent night. But Sophia felt responsible for her. This was going to come up again. One solution would be to accept Duane's invitations. He was certainly available. She sighed. Why wasn't the idea more appealing? Brandon's darkly handsome face appeared before her.

Misty squeezed her eyelids tightly shut to banish the image. Brandon was an improbable dream. She had fallen in love with a man who didn't exist.

She awoke from a deep sleep feeling refreshed, except for the fact that she was ravenous. Voices from the living room told her Warren had arrived. It sounded as though he and Sophia were having a drink. Hopefully her aunt had ordered hors d'oeuvres to go with them. Misty put on a caftan and went out to join them.

"I was just about to go in and see if you were all right," Sophia said. "You've been asleep for hours."

"I guess I was more tired than I realized."

"A drink will wake you up," Warren said. "What can I fix you?"

"Nothing right now, thanks." Misty looked at the cocktail table. It held only a bowl of flowers, a marble cigarette box and a couple of ashtrays. "No hors d'oeuvres?" she asked her aunt.

"I didn't want to spoil our appetites."

"A pound of pâté and a barrel of shrimp wouldn't put a dent in mine. Do you mind if I order something?"

"The place we're going to has divine food," Sophia warned.

"Please don't start that again," Misty begged.

Sophia looked at Warren, who said, "You're not going to deprive me of the pleasure of escorting two beautiful ladies?"

"That's kind of you, Warren, but I'm not lost and abandoned. I turned down a date for tonight," Misty assured him.

"The young man's loss is my gain," he said with a smile. "I really would appreciate it if you'd join us."

He gave no impression of having been pressured into the invitation. Misty decided that Warren was truly a very nice man. She also realized that the thought of spending a long, boring night alone wasn't wildly appealing.

"I'm not dressed," she said uncertainly.

"We'll wait," he answered.

Misty dressed hurriedly, her spirits rising. She rejoined the other two a short time later, actually looking forward to the evening ahead.

Her expectations were justified at first. The food at the fashionable restaurant was excellent, and Misty did justice to it.

Sophia stared at her in amazement. "I've never seen you eat like this."

Misty grinned. "I'm a growing girl."

"Growing wider, if you keep up this pace."

"Leave her alone," Warren advised. "She doesn't have to watch her figure."

"No one else will either if she eats that dessert," Sophia warned.

"I wish that was all *I* had to worry about." Warren chuckled.

Misty glanced up with her spoon poised over a rich custard and ice cream confection. Warren's face didn't reflect his troubles. He looked as though he was enjoying himself thoroughly. Could he be this relaxed if he had a fugitive son who was in danger of going to prison?

He smiled at her suddenly troubled expression. "Don't let Sophia ruin your appetite."

"You're making me sound like a wicked stepmother," Sophia protested.

He covered her hand with his. "You could never play the part."

The way they smiled at each other caught at Misty's heart.

"You're the most generous, open woman I've ever known," Warren continued. "I told—" He stopped abruptly.

"Go on," Sophia prompted. "What have you been saying about me?"

"I described you in glowing terms to my sons," he finished smoothly.

"I'd love to meet them," Sophia said softly.

His voice deepened. "You will if I can entice you back to Philadelphia."

"It's very possible," she murmured.

Misty felt like excess baggage, but she knew they'd object to her leaving. She glanced around the crowded room hopefully. This was a popular restaurant. If Duane was here with a group, she could join them.

As her eyes swept the room Misty spotted someone she *didn't* want to see. Brandon was sitting at a table for four, with Bootsy and a distinguished-looking older couple. Misty's inadvertent little sound drew her aunt's attention.

Sophia turned to see what she was staring at. "There are the Dedinis!" she exclaimed happily. "And Brandon," she added more quietly, with a quick glance at Misty.

"Don't forget Bootsy," Misty reminded her tautly.

"We must go over and say hello," Sophia declared. "It will be nice for both of you to meet the Dedinis before their party."

How could she even suggest such a humiliating thing! "I'll wait here for you," Misty said coldly as Warren rose from his chair.

"You'll come with us," Sophia answered firmly. She lowered her voice for Misty's ears alone. "I told you life offers no guarantees. I'm aware of how you feel, but a niece of mine shows grace under pressure."

Misty stood up slowly. Sophia was right of course. She mustn't give Brandon the satisfaction of knowing he'd hurt her. But it was going to be the hardest thing she'd ever done.

Brandon and the count stood politely when they reached their table. As everyone exchanged greetings, Brandon gave Misty a melting smile.

"I missed you," he murmured.

Anger so intense that it made her dizzy raced through Misty. She turned pointedly to Bootsy. "Have you heard anything about your ring?"

The beautiful blonde's mouth was sulky. "The police say they're working on it, but they're all a bunch of incompetents. They couldn't catch a little old lady on crutches if they were on roller skates."

"I hope the ring was insured at least." Misty didn't care one way or the other, but it kept her from looking at Brandon.

"The insurance company is as bad as the police," Bootsy complained. "Try being late with a premium and see what happens. But when it comes to paying off a claim, they suddenly get writer's cramp. Didn't you have the same experience?" she asked the countess.

As the two women discussed their mutual trials and tribulations, Misty was momentarily alone with Brandon.

"What's wrong, honey?" he asked softly.

She was almost struck dumb by his colossal effrontery. Almost, but not quite. "What makes you think anything is wrong?" she asked icily.

He chuckled. "I know that famous temper of yours. You're ready to go off like a skyrocket."

"What would I have to be angry about?" she asked through gritted teeth.

"The same thing that's frustrating me," he said huskily. "You don't know how much I wanted to see you today."

"You must really think I'm simpleminded!" She fought to keep her fury under control. "How often do you think I'll fall for that line?"

"If there were any way I could have gotten away, I would have, but I was completely tied up."

Misty glanced over at Bootsy. "So I see," she said bitterly. "Did you take her to the inn? It seems to inspire you."

Brandon's fingers bit into her arm. "How can you even suggest such a thing? I told you how I felt in my note."

She yanked her arm away. "What note?"

"The one I sent with the flowers."

"I never got either one."

Brandon swore pungently. "I'll skin that florist alive!"

"Misty, you haven't met the Dedinis yet." Sophia claimed her attention. "Anna, Marcello, this is my niece, Misty."

"Such a pleasure, my dear. We're so fond of your aunt."

Through a haze of anger, Misty inspected the elegantly groomed older woman. Even in her distracted state she noticed that the countess was beautifully dressed and bedecked with exquisite jewelry.

"We're so happy you'll be here for our little party," Anna Dedini continued.

"It was kind of you to invite me," Misty answered automatically.

"Well, we've kept you gentlemen standing long enough," Sophia said.

"Won't you join us?" the count asked. "We can move to a larger table."

"We've already finished dinner, and we're going on to Numero Uno," Sophia replied. "It's a new disco in the Excelsior."

"That sounds entertaining," the countess said. "Have coffee with us, and we'll all go together."

Sophia hesitated, but Misty didn't. She'd been as graceful under pressure as she intended to be. A little more and her boiler would explode!

"I'm sure my aunt and Warren would be delighted, but I'm meeting someone," she said firmly.

Brandon caught up with her before she got to the door. "Misty, I have to talk to you," he said urgently.

"We have nothing to say to each other—now, or at any other time." With her head held high she swept out the door, confident that he couldn't follow her.

Misty's triumph turned to ashes in the taxi going back to the hotel. She had salvaged her pride, but Bootsy had wound up with Brandon.

How could it hurt so much? He was deceitful, manipulative, untrustworthy—and that was just for starters! For all she knew, he might even be a criminal. How could she still ache for the touch of his hands, the imprint of his mouth? Misty rested her head on the back of the seat and closed her eyes in despair.

The first thing she saw when she walked into the suite was a huge vase of deep red roses. Misty's breath caught in her throat. Had Brandon been telling the truth? Two notes were tucked into the foliage. One was sealed in a white envelope. The other was a folded piece of hotel stationery.

She read that one first. It said: These flowers arrived for Miss Carlysle this morning and were unfortunately misdirected. The management deeply regrets the error and hopes it didn't cause any inconvenience.

A sound somewhere between tears and laughter escaped from Misty's throat. No inconvenience if you didn't count the fact that this was the worst day of her entire life. Her fingers were shaking as she tore open the white envelope.

Brandon's note read:

Darling Misty, yesterday was as close to heaven as I want to get as long as you're here on earth. I ache to hold you and kiss you, to take up where we left off. Unfortunately, I can't be with you until tomorrow. I received a lead on Robby that will take me out of town for the day, and tonight I have to see Bootsy about some information she has. Wait for me, sweetheart, and know that I'll be thinking of you every minute.

It was signed, Love, Brandon.

Misty stared at the ending, her heart pounding. Did he really mean it, or was it just a conventional way to end a message? But there was nothing conventional about his words! As she read them again, all the misery of that long day dissolved. Brandon did care! She should have had more faith.

How could she have lashed out at him like that? No wonder he looked puzzled and hurt. But it wasn't really her fault, given the circumstances. Misty couldn't wait to explain. She knew how painful rejection could be.

For a moment she considered tracking him down at Numero Uno, then discarded the idea. They wouldn't be able to talk with the others there. Frustrating as it was, she would have to wait for tomorrow.

Misty was too keyed up to go to bed. After her long nap she wouldn't have been able to sleep, anyway. She wandered through the suite for a while, then decided to get undressed. Even if she couldn't sleep, reading in bed might take her mind off the endless hours she had to get through before seeing Brandon.

She was pulling a pale blue chiffon nightgown over her head when someone knocked at the door to the living room. Her heart skipped a beat at the unexpected sound. Could it be Brandon? Or was that just wishful thinking? He couldn't very well get away from the others that early. Bootsy, especially, liked to party till dawn.

Steeling herself against disappointment, Misty hurriedly pulled on a robe and went to the door. When she looked through the peephole, incredulous joy gripped her. Brandon was standing in the hall. Even the grim look on his face was beautiful!

He strode into the living room and turned to scowl at her. "Okay, now what's this all about?"

"I thought you were going to a disco," she said softly.

"Never mind that! What did you mean by those things you said to me?"

"It was all a misunderstanding, Brandon. When I didn't hear from you, I—"

"You went up in smoke because I didn't phone?" he interrupted violently. "I explained why I couldn't."

"But I didn't get your note!"

He looked pointedly at the bouquet on the coffee table. "You also claimed you didn't get my flowers."

Wordlessly she handed him the message from the manager.

His scowl deepened as he read it. "I ought to beat that incompetent clown to a pulp!" he swore.

"You can see how I'd be upset," Misty pleaded. "You were very... attentive... yesterday, and then today you didn't even phone. What was I supposed to think?"

"Not what you did!"

"Be reasonable, Brandon. You would have felt pretty rejected yourself."

He clasped her in his arms then and held her fiercely. "How could you possibly have doubted the way I felt about you? Didn't I show you in every way I knew how?"

Misty's very bones seemed to liquefy at the memory of Brandon's stirring caresses the length of her nude body. "I'm sorry for the things I said," she murmured.

"You damn well should be!" he answered sternly, although his expression had softened.

"Will you forgive me?"

"I'm willing to negotiate." He scooped her up in his arms and carried her to the couch. "What are you ready to do as penance?"

"Anything you say."

His eyes gleamed as he gazed down into her lovely face. "That's a reckless offer. How do you know I won't take advantage of your generosity?"

"I trust you," she whispered.

"My darling Misty!"

Brandon's mouth sought hers urgently, his kiss expressing pent-up longing. While his tongue probed deeply, his hands caressed her body, as though he wanted to experience every inch of her.

Misty was flooded by the same desire. She ran her fingers through his hair and traced the contours of his face to be sure he was real. After her hopelessness earlier, this seemed like a dream.

Brandon finally dragged his mouth away and buried his face in her neck. "This is all I thought about since I left you yesterday," he muttered. "Did you feel the same way, sweetheart?"

Her laughter had a little catch in it. "You can't imagine how I felt—especially when I saw you tonight with Bootsy."

Brandon raised his head and sighed. "She's a necessary evil, I'm afraid."

"What could she know about Robby?" Misty asked in a small voice. In spite of everything, she couldn't help feeling insecure about the glamorous blonde. "He couldn't have taken her ring. If he were there that night, you would have seen him."

"He didn't pull the actual robbery, but he might have been an accomplice. Or it could be someone else entirely. Someone above reproach who's masterminding these thefts while everyone looks for a criminal type."

"Do you have any clues at all to the man's identity?"

Brandon hesitated for an instant. "I have a few suspicions," he replied in a peculiarly flat tone of voice.

"I hope you're right about the thief being someone other than Robby. That would be a relief for Warren."

Brandon stared down at her with mixed emotions warring on his strong face. A groan was wrenched out of him as his arms tightened almost painfully.

"I don't want to talk about robberies or jewel thieves. I want to carry you off and make love to you all night and all day."

Misty had been about to ask why he thought Bootsy could help him find the accomplice, but when Brandon lifted her in his arms and started for the bedroom, it seemed supremely unimportant.

Chapter Eight

The bedroom was in semidarkness, lit only by a small lamp on the bedside table. It cast shadows over Brandon's face as he lowered Misty gently to her feet, giving him a predatory male expression. The avid gleam in his green eyes reinforced the impression.

She shivered with excitement, but Brandon misunderstood. "Don't be timid with me, darling. I want you to come to me without reservations."

"I don't have any." Her face was tender as she gazed up at him.

He parted her robe and put his arms around her waist, gathering her so close that she could feel the rapid beat of his heart. Only the thin chiffon nightgown shielded her body from his tensile strength. He was so taut that she could sense the leashed power he was holding in check.

"I can't believe this is finally happening," he muttered.

Misty felt a sense of power at his rigid reserve. She laughed softly, pushing his jacket off his shoulders. After removing his tie, she began to unbutton his shirt.

"You couldn't get away now if you tried," she murmured.

A tremor ran through him as she pulled his shirt out of his slacks and then smoothed her palms over his chest. His muscles contracted under her suggestive caress.

"Why would I want to?" he asked huskily. "I've dreamed about this moment from the first time I saw you."

He slipped a lacy strap off her shoulder and freed one rounded breast. It was Misty's turn to quiver as he slowly caressed the firm mound. Her excitement mounted when he rotated the rosy tip with his thumb.

"I knew we'd make love, and I knew it would be wonderful," he said deeply.

Misty was melting in the inferno created by his hands, his voice, the promise of his hard body. She closed her eyes to savor the pleasure. When his lips trailed a path of burning kisses over her breast, the pleasure escalated into molten desire.

"That feels so..." Her voice trailed away.

"Tell me, darling. Don't be shy. Let yourself go with me."

He slipped the other strap off her shoulder, and the gown slid over the contours of her body, almost in slow motion. Brandon watched as both breasts were uncovered, then the flat plane of her stomach, and finally her long, tapering thighs. His eyes were almost incandescent as he gazed at the slender perfection of her form.

"My God, you're beautiful." It was almost like a prayer.

He touched her, starting at her slim shoulders and continuing past her hips. The erotic feeling intensified when he retraced the path with his lips, pausing where she was most vulnerable.

When he knelt before her, clasping her hips and carrying on his devastation, Misty's knees buckled. "I never felt this out of control before," she moaned.

Brandon lifted her in his arms and carried her to the bed. "Yes, my love, this is the way it's supposed to be, wild and free."

That was the way she felt. Clasping her arms around his neck, she plunged her tongue into his mouth and urged her body against his. All inhibitions were gone. She was a woman in love, following her deepest instincts.

Brandon was ignited by her fire. He flung off the rest of his clothes and clasped her against his hardened body. His careful restraint was burned away in the flames that consumed them both.

"I can't wait any longer." His tortured words were muffled against her skin.

"I don't want you to," she answered urgently.

Misty welcomed Brandon's possession, arching her body to meet his thrusts. He filled the aching void that was tormenting her, guiding her into a spiral of throbbing sensation that was almost unbearably thrilling. Every straining muscle tightened as she struggled toward an ultimate goal. Release came in a cresting wave that broke with an awesome power.

When he felt her tension relax, Brandon allowed his own satisfaction. Misty felt the surge of power as he reached fulfillment and then collapsed against her. She held him as he traveled his descent, experiencing a rush of tenderness. Brandon had guaranteed her own pleasure before taking his.

They were quiet in each other's arms, savoring the aftermath of love. Both were completely sated.

Brandon was the first to stir. He smoothed the damp hair away from Misty's face. "Did I tell you that you're wonderful?" he asked tenderly.

"I wouldn't mind hearing it again," she answered softly.

"You're the most beautiful woman in the world. You brighten my days and gladden my nights." He punctuated each statement with a kiss.

She touched his mouth lovingly. "That's very poetic."

"You make me feel that way. I didn't know it could ever be like this."

"Does that mean I'll have a special place in your memory?" she asked wistfully.

Brandon had brought her ecstasy beyond belief. He had lavished tributes on her and treated her with tender care—but he hadn't said he loved her. Maybe his love was too much to ask for, but as passion diminished to a warm glow of contentment, Misty desperately wanted some sign that she held a cherished place in his heart.

Brandon stroked her body lazily. "I intend to refresh my memory often."

"Don't I have anything to say about it?" In spite of her effort to sound joking, her voice held a slight edge.

"I was hoping you'd agree." He raised up on one elbow and looked down at her searchingly. "What's the matter, darling? Are you having regrets?"

"You know I'm not."

"Then what is it? I can tell something's troubling you. Did I disappoint you in some way?"

"You never could." She smiled to reassure him.

He continued to look doubtful. "I wanted it to be as earth-shattering for you as it was for me."

Misty put her arms around his neck and curved her body into his. "It was. Couldn't you tell?"

"I hoped so." He held her close, stroking her back with sensual pleasure. "You mean so much to me, angel."

"Tell me how much." She almost stopped breathing, waiting for his answer.

"I look forward to seeing you, and I'm frustrated when I can't. I resent all the people and circumstances that keep us apart. I'd like to close a door and shut everyone out of our lives."

It wasn't a declaration of love, but his response was very satisfying. If Brandon felt that way, surely a meaningful relationship would develop between them. If only there were more time!

"We both have obligations to other people," she said. "We'll have to settle for whatever time we can manage together."

"I'm tired of other people. I don't want to share you."

"You're the one who's always involved," she pointed out.

"I know." He sighed.

"Why don't you come with us when we leave Rome?" she asked impulsively.

Brandon's hands stilled for a moment, then resumed their gentle caressing. "I can't imagine Rome without you."

That wasn't an answer—or was it? Misty was afraid to press the point. She was even sorry she'd brought it up. Why spoil this idyllic moment?

He cupped her chin in his palm and gazed at her with some unreadable emotion. "Let's make the most of the present, sweetheart. No one knows what the future will bring."

Her heart plummeted as she realized what he was saying. This was all there was going to be. She looked searchingly into his intense face, memorizing every beloved feature.

"I'll never forget you, Brandon," she whispered.

His hand tightened. "Hey, that sounds like goodbye."

She swallowed the lump in her throat and forced a smile. At least she could play her part gracefully. "I didn't want to wait till the last minute."

He frowned. "You could leave me without a backward glance?"

"I asked you to come with me."

"And if I can't, that's it?" he asked harshly.

Misty moved out of his arms and sat up against the headboard, pulling the sheet over her bare breasts. "Don't make me the heavy. You're the one who doesn't want to get involved. You can go anywhere you like, whenever you like—if you wanted to."

His expression changed subtly. "No one can do exactly as he pleases."

"You have been," she challenged.

He hesitated. "I'm not proud of my life-style lately. I hope to change it soon."

The tight band around Misty's chest burst as she understood Brandon's reluctance to commit himself. "You're going home?"

"As soon as I wind things up here."

"Oh, Brandon, I'm so happy!"

"Even if it means that you'll be in Europe while I'm in Philadelphia?"

"I won't be for long. We can write to each other."

"That's a pretty pale substitute for what we have now." He reached out and pulled her back into his arms. "I can't give you up."

Misty's mind was working furiously. If Brandon asked her to go with him, she would. Sophia would be upset, but this vacation had already delivered all the romance she'd promised!

"When do you expect to leave?" she asked breathlessly.

"I'm not sure. I hope a week will do it."

"Have you spoken to your father?"

"My father?" His blank expression changed to a guarded one. "No, this is strictly my decision."

That sounded as though the senior Mr. Powers was reserving judgment. But this time Brandon wasn't taking the line of least resistance. Misty felt a fierce joy that he finally intended to take charge of his own life, even if it meant giving up a fortune.

"Will you go back to the bank when you return home?" she asked.

"Probably not."

"What will you do?"

He smiled at her anxious face. "Don't you think a big strapping fellow like me can get a job?"

"Of course I do! I just . . . well, I worry about you."

"Don't worry, angel." He kissed the tip of her nose. "I'm like a cat. I always land on my feet."

"I know, but if you need a place to stay, you can use my apartment in New York."

"What happens when you come home?"

"Well, if you haven't found anything by then, you can, uh, stay on until you do."

He laughed softly. "With that incentive, I don't think I'd look very hard."

"I really mean it," she said earnestly. "You wouldn't be committed in any way."

His fingers trailed erotic circles over her breast. "Unless you call making love every night and every morning a commitment."

"I wouldn't expect it," she said faintly as a familiar warmth started to spread through her midsection.

"But I would." His legs scissored around hers, pinning her body to the juncture of his loins. "You're so sweet, my darling."

As his mouth touched hers, voices sounded in the living room.

Misty stiffened in alarm. Suppose Sophia came in to say good-night? They would both be terribly embarrassed, and it would cheapen something that was very beautiful.

Brandon understood instantly. "Don't panic, angel," he murmured.

With a lithe movement he slid noiselessly out of bed. Misty watched with regret as he dressed swiftly. His lean body was just a fluid shadow in the dim room, moving with pantherlike grace.

"I can't believe this is happening to us again," she whispered helplessly.

Brandon's voice was rich with suppressed laughter. "The army could use your aunt's built-in radar system."

"I know." Misty sighed.

"Tomorrow we're going to outwit them all. Be ready at ten in the morning."

"Where are we going?"

"I'll tell you then." He reached under the covers to caress her warm body while he kissed her lingeringly. When Misty made a small sound of appreciation he lifted his head and murmured, "I love you, sweetheart."

Before she could react he was gone. The door to the hall opened silently, a slice of light illuminated her stunned face for an instant, and then she was alone.

Had she heard correctly? Did Brandon really say he loved her? As realization set in she felt like laughing and crying, like getting up and dancing around the room. Her most impossible dream had come true! Brandon loved her!

Misty's eyelashes fluttered onto her flushed cheeks as the bedroom door opened quietly from the living room. She couldn't talk to anyone at that moment and make sense. It would take time to get used to this incredible turn of events!

After a brief look at her still form, Sophia closed the door again. "I guess she's asleep," she said to Warren. "Poor dear, I'm afraid she didn't have a very good time tonight."

Misty was ready and waiting when Brandon came to pick her up the next morning. Her eyes were shining like twin stars, although she'd slept very little.

He hadn't told her where they were going, so she hadn't known what to wear. She'd settled for a yellow knit suit with a yellow and white print blouse that lent softness to the straight skirt and boxy jacket.

Her first impulse on seeing Brandon was to ask if he'd really meant what he said the night before, but diffidence set in. "Am I dressed all right?" she asked instead.

"You look fantastic."

The male look of appreciation on his face was very satisfying, but Misty felt curiously constrained. In his expensive cashmere jacket and carelessly knotted ascot, Brandon looked like a member of Sophia's world, not hers. Was this really the man who had lost all control in her arms the night before?

"You didn't say where we were going," she commented nervously.

His eyes lit with laughter. "We were rather short of time." As her color rose he took her in his arms. "Today's going to be different."

All of Misty's shyness fled. This was reality; the rest was just window dressing. "I couldn't sleep last night," she whispered.

"That makes two of us." His lips trailed across her cheek. "I kept remembering how you felt in my arms."

Sophia's bedroom door opened, and she came out wearing a glamorous pink satin robe. Her usual graciousness was missing as she viewed their close embrace.

"You do get around, Brandon," she remarked dryly.

"Good morning, Sophia." He released Misty without embarrassment.

"Brandon and I are going out for the day," Misty said quickly.

"Really?" Sophia gazed impassively at her. "I'd like to speak to you for a moment first."

He looked amused as Misty followed her aunt into the bedroom.

Sophia didn't beat around the bush. "I'd rather you didn't go out with Brandon today. In fact, I'd prefer that you don't accept any future invitations from him."

"Why?" Misty stared at her in bewilderment. "I thought you liked him."

"I do, but he isn't right for you."

"When did you decide that?"

Sophia chose her words carefully. "I'm the first one to admit that Brandon is fascinating. That's the problem.

He's *too* fascinating. He could charm a miser out of his millions."

"Have you decided he's a fortune hunter after all? There's just one hitch. I don't happen to have millions."

"I wasn't implying anything like that. I'm just trying to tell you that he's out of your league. He has a different life-style, a more liberal way of looking at things."

"You aren't making sense. What happened to all that stuff about not judging people, and taking them as they are?"

Sophia sighed. "I didn't want to tell you this, but you leave me no other choice. Brandon is the worst kind of womanizer. You saw him with Bootsy last night."

"She's neither quantity nor quality," Misty said disdainfully.

"Let me finish. He started out with her, but that's not the way the evening ended."

Misty gave her aunt a startled look. "What do you mean?"

"After you left we went on to Numero Uno and ran into Jacqueline with another group. She made a concentrated play for Brandon."

"That must have rattled Bootsy's cage," Misty said with satisfaction.

"It was ghastly! I thought they were going to get physical. Anyway, Brandon settled the whole thing. He made some lame excuse and left. Bootsy stayed on with us, but Jacqueline left soon after."

The corners of Misty's mouth twitched. "You think he had a prearranged date to meet Jacqueline?"

"Don't be naïve, darling. What other explanation could there be?"

Misty's smile was enchanting. "He might have one that would surprise you."

Sophia looked at her with a troubled expression. "I blame myself for this whole thing. I was the one who advised you to encourage Brandon. I thought he'd bring a little color and excitement into your life. I realized that he might be too experienced for you, but I had no idea the man has the morals of a tomcat."

"Don't you think you're convicting him on very flimsy evidence?"

"I wouldn't judge him at all if he wasn't trying to add your scalp to his collection. Bootsy and Jacqueline know the score, but I'm afraid you'll believe the line he hands out. I can just imagine how seductive he can be."

Misty didn't think Sophia's imagination could possibly do Brandon justice, yet telling her so would only prolong the argument. It would also be pointless to reveal that he was in love with her. Her aunt would merely believe it was his technique for bedding down women who resisted his other approaches.

"We'll have to save this discussion for later," she said. "Brandon's waiting for me."

"You haven't listened to a word I said!"

"Yes, I have. I just don't have time right now to convince you how wrong you are."

"Will you at least promise to think about what I told you?" Sophia pleaded. "I don't want you to do something you'll regret."

Misty's smile was radiant. "That's one thing you don't have to worry about."

Brandon was idly leafing through a magazine when they returned. He looked up quizzically. "Any problems?"

"That depends on whom you're asking," Sophia said grimly.

Misty picked up her purse hastily. "I'll see you later."

"When will you be back?" her aunt persisted.

Brandon was the one who answered. "Probably late."

Sophia watched with a stony expression as they walked out the door.

"Am I wrong, or did I just get dropped from your aunt's top ten list of favorites?" he asked as they waited for the elevator.

"She's suspicious of you."

"In what way?" He was suddenly wary.

"Sophia indicated that you could give Casanova lessons in seduction." Misty laughed. "I could have told her she was right, but I didn't want to upset her further."

Brandon's face didn't reflect her amusement. "Did I seduce you last night, Misty?"

"What do you think?" she asked softly.

"I'd like to think you wanted me as much as I wanted you."

"If you couldn't tell, then I must have been doing something wrong," she murmured as they entered the elevator and began their descent.

His rigid pose relaxed, and his voice dropped to a husky register. "The only disappointment last night was when I had to leave you."

"I wish it didn't have to be this way, but Sophia wouldn't understand." Misty sighed.

Brandon put his arm around her shoulders and led her across the lobby. "You're her niece, and she wants to protect you. That's understandable. Sophia doesn't know we share the same goal."

"I don't need to be taken care of," Misty protested. "I'm an adult woman."

He chuckled. "You won't get any arguments out of me."

The attendant brought Brandon's car, curtailing their conversation. When they drove away, Misty's attention was distracted by the fascinating pattern of Rome. She looked at the smartly dressed parade of pedestrians, both men and women. Everyone seemed to have some urgent destination. Their faces were intent, their manner assured.

"Except for the glorious, old world buildings, this reminds me a little bit of New York," Misty commented.

"I suppose all big cities have something in common."

Misty laughed. "You're right. I don't drive in New York City, either."

"Put yourself in my hands and enjoy the scenery," he advised.

She watched his competent handling of the car in the snarl of traffic. Brandon inspired confidence. She knew instinctively that he could handle any situation. When he turned his head and smiled at her, Misty's heart soared. She would trust him with her life.

"Hang on, we'll be out of this mess soon," he said, capturing her hand.

"Where are we going?" she asked.

"Where would you like to go?"

"Anywhere with you," she answered simply.

His hand tightened as he turned his head to gaze at her with glowing eyes. "If you keep looking at me like that, we might not get there."

The apoplectic honking of the driver in back of them put an end to the tender moment. Their longing turned to laughter.

When the traffic thinned and they reached the outskirts of the city, Misty suddenly knew their destination.

"How did you know I wanted to go back to the inn?" she asked with a catch in her voice.

He carried her hand to his mouth and kissed the palm. "We left something unfinished."

Neither spoke much on the scenic drive. The things they had to say to each other were too precious to be tossed off casually. Misty's fingers were curled into her palm, guarding Brandon's kiss like a talisman.

The proprietor of the inn greeted them like old friends. He was delighted to give them the room they'd occupied before, at Brandon's request.

When the man left, Brandon put out the Do Not Disturb sign.

Misty's cheeks were very pink. "It's only eleven in the morning," she murmured.

His soft laughter had a stirring, male sound. "I know. Half the day is over. We should have left earlier."

Her body tingled with anticipation as he moved closer. The momentary shyness she'd felt evaporated. "We're here now," she whispered.

"I can hardly believe it—no other people, no interruptions." He took her in his arms and held her tightly. "I'd like to keep you here forever."

Misty pulled his ascot out of the open neck of his shirt and slowly untied it. "I wouldn't be hard to convince."

His answer was stilled as she unbuttoned his shirt and rubbed her cheek against the dark mat of hair that cushioned his hard chest. A shudder ran through Brandon as she slid her hand around his waist and slipped her fingers inside his waistband.

He arched his back as she moved her palm sensuously over the tight curves of his buttocks. Reaching back, he caught her wrist in a viselike grip.

"Go easy, little one," he gasped. "I'm not made of steel."

Misty could tell that. His body was taut, yet warm and yielding under her fingers. She wanted to touch him everywhere, to discover every hidden secret of his thrilling male body. Using her free hand, she unbuckled his belt.

"Please, darling!" His voice was hoarse. "You're pushing my self-control to the limit. I want to bring *you* this kind of pleasure."

Misty smiled into his anguished eyes. "You are, my love."

After staring at her rapt face, Brandon released her wrist. It took a great effort, but he offered no resistance as she removed his clothing, piece by piece. Even when she gazed at every portion of his body, Brandon maintained his statuelike pose. But when Misty stroked his loins and leaned forward to touch his flat male nipple with the tip of her tongue, his control snapped.

"A man can only take so much," he growled.

Her clothing fell away in a blur of motion as he tugged at snaps and zippers. Her fragile bra and panties joined the heap on the floor. Brandon was like a man possessed. Until she stood slender and nude before him. Then his frenzied movements turned to gentle caresses.

"You're like an ivory goddess," he breathed, feathering his fingertips over her entire body.

Misty moved closer, staring up at him with luminous eyes. "Shall I show you how human I am?"

He reached for her convulsively. His mouth devoured hers while he made little wordless sounds that indicated his hunger. Their bodies were joined as closely as their lips, but it still wasn't close enough. Misty burrowed deeper, scorching herself at the heat that was emanating from his loins.

"You're like a fever in my blood," he muttered. "I can't get enough of you."

He covered her face with kisses and continued down her neck, stopping to nip at the delicate cord. Misty tilted her head back, feeling the flames rising higher.

"Love me, darling," she begged. "Love me now."

"Yes, angel, now!"

Brandon carried her to the bed. His dark head remained poised over hers for a stirring instant while he drank in the naked passion on her face. Then he lowered his body.

Misty felt a piercing joy that escalated with each thrusting movement, each fevered act. She clutched him desperately as the rhythmic cycle carried her higher and higher. Brandon was at the center of her universe. Only he could deliver her from the storm that was gathering force inside her. When the turbulence climaxed and brought peace to her throbbing body, his name was on her lips.

Their heartbeats diminished slowly in the quiet aftermath. Brandon rolled over onto his side, taking her with him. Both felt languid and fulfilled.

After a while he kissed her eyelids tenderly. "You're ruining my reputation as an experienced lover," he murmured.

She opened her eyes to gaze at his beloved face. "How can you say that?"

"I planned to make love to you for hours, but I couldn't resist you—either last night or today."

Misty smiled enchantingly. "I don't have any complaints."

"You shouldn't have, since it was your fault," he said with mock severity. "Where did you learn to seduce a man like that?"

"I never have before. You bring out my hidden talents."

"See that I'm the only one who does," he ordered.

"I could say the same thing to you." Misty couldn't help thinking about Bootsy and Jacqueline and all the ones she didn't even know about.

Brandon chuckled. "That's an easy promise to make."

"Even though your two current women were fighting over you last night?"

"You're my current woman," he said throatily.

Misty stirred in his embrace. "I don't think I like that."

"No, you're right. How could I have said such a thing?" He pulled her close again. "You're my *only* woman. The one I love with all my heart and soul."

"Oh, Brandon, that's what I needed to hear." She put her arms around his neck and pressed her lips to his throat. "You don't know how miserable those two dragon ladies have made me."

"They aren't even in your league, sweetheart." He stroked her hair lovingly.

"But they're so aggressive. They don't make any secret of wanting you. That must be very flattering to a man."

"It is." His hand moved sensuously over her bare body. "You excite and delight me."

"We were talking about Bootsy and Jacqueline."

"Why?" He cupped her breast and bent his head to kiss the stiffening tip.

At that moment Misty couldn't think of a reason. It was only much later, after they had made love once more and then fallen asleep in each other's arms, that their names came up again. But not immediately.

She opened her eyes to find Brandon staring at her.

"What are you thinking about?" she asked softly.

"Lunch," he answered unexpectedly. "We didn't have any."

"That's not very romantic!"

He grinned. "I have to conserve my energy. You've used up most of it."

"Can you think of a better cause?"

"There isn't one." He kissed her very satisfactorily. "Aren't you hungry?"

"Starved," she admitted. "I didn't even have breakfast."

"Then lunch is very definitely in order." He got up and called room service, then climbed back into bed.

"Shouldn't we get dressed?" Misty asked tentatively.

"Don't even think of it. I'm not letting you out of this bed until it's time to go back."

"I wish we didn't have to," she said wistfully. "Go back, I mean."

"I'm available," he answered promptly.

"How would I explain it to Sophia?"

"You could tell her we love each other and want to be together. She's a very sophisticated lady. She'd understand."

Misty shook her head. "You saw how she was today. Sophia is convinced that you're stringing along half the women in Rome."

"I don't know whether to be flattered or annoyed."

"If you'd let me tell her the truth about Bootsy, she'd be more understanding."

"No!" Brandon modified his sharp answer. "It isn't my secret to tell."

"Maybe Warren will tell her, and then you'll be off the hook."

"I wouldn't put it past him." Brandon's face was unexpectedly grim.

"Well, at least Sophia wouldn't judge you so harshly. She thought you ducked out on Bootsy last night to meet Jacqueline. What kind of excuse did you give that aroused her suspicions?"

Brandon grinned mischievously. "I said I had a headache."

"You didn't!"

"We're supposed to have equality between the sexes, aren't we? You women have been getting away with that line for years."

"No wonder she jumped to conclusions. Couldn't you have thought of a better excuse?"

"Not at the moment. You had me tied up in knots. All I wanted to do was see you and straighten out whatever was wrong."

As they gazed at each other, remembering how they'd settled their differences, the room service waiter knocked on the door.

Misty ran into the bathroom and tossed a bathrobe out to Brandon. While the waiter was bringing in their lunch, she slipped into the other robe and smoothed her tousled hair.

The open-faced sandwiches were less elaborate than their former hot lunch, but equally delicious. A selection of smoked sturgeon, Italian ham and several cheeses were served on a variety of breads. Accompanying them were both pasta and fresh fruit salads, the latter topped with sour cream and honey.

Misty and Brandon were too busy eating to talk much at first. It wasn't until they started on the crisp cookies stuffed with mocha cream that Brandon returned to the subject they'd been discussing.

"Sophia will have to know about us sooner or later. I intend to spend as much time with you as possible."

"She'll come around when she sees how we feel about each other," Misty assured him.

"I hope so." Brandon put down his cookie and gave her a troubled look. "Promise you won't let her whisk you away suddenly without telling me."

"Sophia wouldn't leave before the Dedini ball. She's looking forward to it."

His face became guarded. "It's just another party."

"Not according to Sophia."

"Did she say why?"

"It's going to be a big bash. As I understand it, people will be flying in from all over the world."

"That must be old hat to Sophia. She's traveled the party trail for a good many years."

"But maybe not for much longer," Misty said soberly.

"Why not?"

"Nothing is forever," she answered evasively.

"Don't tell me she's getting tired of the rat race." Brandon's voice was faintly derisive. "What's she going to do, settle down in suburbia?"

"Maybe she intends to go to work," Misty answered evenly.

"There aren't very many jobs that give three hours off for lunch."

"People like you who were born with a silver spoon in their mouths think everything is a joke," Misty flared. "Well, let me tell you, Sophia is the most gallant woman I've ever known."

"I wasn't criticizing your aunt, honey. I like Sophia. I was just pointing out the limitations of a job. It isn't the lark it sounds like. She has no idea how the have-nots live."

The necessity of defending her aunt outweighed other considerations. Sophia's situation would be common knowledge soon, anyway, and Misty wanted Brandon to understand. They were the two people she loved most.

"You asked me to keep a secret; now I'm asking you to keep one," she said. "Everyone thinks Sophia is independently wealthy, but she isn't. This stay at the Eden is her last fling."

Brandon stared at her blankly for a moment. "But her clothes, her jewels..."

"She's very clever about clothes, and the jewels are fake."

His face was a mixture of emotions as he absorbed this information. "So that's why she's not worried about being robbed."

Misty smiled wryly. "It's a blessing in a way. Most people can't tell the difference, but Sophia says a professional jewel thief can."

Brandon's expression was impassive. "If she's fooled everyone all this time, why stop now?"

"She can't afford to keep up the pretense anymore. Sophia's jewels were once real. They were almost all her husband left her, but for his sake she didn't want anyone to know. She sold off her jewelry little by little and lived on the proceeds. But now she's scraping the bottom of the barrel. I'm telling you this because I want you to appreciate her loyalty to the people she loves, and to understand why I could never hurt her."

Brandon was gripped by strong emotion. He got up from the table and took Misty in his arms. "You're quite a family, sweetheart."

"You do understand, don't you?" she pleaded.

"More than you realize," he muttered, burying his face in her hair.

Chapter Nine

Misty soon had second thoughts about having confided in Brandon. Although his physical response was satisfactory, he seemed distracted. The change had occurred after she told him about Sophia.

Was Brandon what she'd first suspected, a fortune hunter? Every instinct demanded rejection of the idea. He loved her! Hadn't he just demonstrated that? But the demons of doubt started to taunt her.

A consummate lover like Brandon could say all the right words automatically. Especially if a lot of money was involved. Sophia had nobody in the world but Misty. She could reasonably be expected to leave a fortune to her—if she had one.

Misty pushed her chair back abruptly and stood up. "I'm going to take a shower."

"Okay, honey," he answered absently.

In spite of her efforts, Misty's thoughts were somber as she stood under the pelting water. Would Brandon suggest going back to the city now, or would he play out the charade? No! She mustn't let herself believe that.

Her eyes were closed when the shower curtain was pulled aside. She opened them to see him stepping into the tub.

"What are you doing here?" she asked without thinking.

He chuckled deeply. "I thought you'd like someone to scrub your back."

Misty tried to avoid looking at his lean form. She mustn't let her judgment be clouded by a purely physical reaction. Brandon's naked body was enough to drive everything else out of a woman's mind. His broad torso and long, muscular legs were deeply tanned, calling attention to the narrow strip of white that banded his lean hips. After one quick glance, Misty turned her back.

He soaped a washcloth and started at her shoulders. "Did you know you have freckles?"

"Nobody's perfect," she answered with forced flippancy.

"You are." The cloth glided down her spine. "I can't find a flaw anywhere."

"How about the freckles?" She caught her breath as he smoothed her buttocks.

"Those are beauty spots." He turned her around and began soaping her breasts with gentle circular movements.

"That's enough!" she gasped, grabbing for the washcloth.

He laughed softly, thwarting her efforts. "I like to finish what I start."

She was powerless to stop him as he continued down her body in a slow progress that was almost unbearably erotic. When he reached her hips, Brandon squatted down and lifted her foot onto his knee. She uttered a tiny sound, somewhere between protest and pleasure, as the cloth slid over her calf and up her thigh.

His eyes blazed with green fire as he dropped the washcloth and rinsed her sensitized skin with his hands. Misty's legs started to tremble when he caressed her inner thigh, moving inexorably upward.

"You're so soft and warm," he murmured. "I love to touch you."

When he stroked her intimately, Misty anchored her fingers in his thick hair to keep her balance. She was breathing rapidly. Brandon deepened his exploration, staring up at her with molten passion on his face.

"Do you know how it makes me feel to see you respond like this? To know I can bring you pleasure?"

"I never knew there could be this much pleasure," she whispered.

"You make it all happen, my love." He stood up and took her in his arms, making her aware of his masculinity. "I reach the heights with you."

He kissed her tenderly, then with growing urgency as Misty moved against him in a restless demand for completion. The chain reaction Brandon had started was building to an explosion. She was filled with a throbbing sensation that grew in intensity as he fed the flames inside her. When he sensed that she had reached the outer limits of endurance, he completed their union.

The warm water was like a sensual caress on their twined bodies, thousands of tiny fingers massaging them erotically. Misty climbed Brandon's heights in his arms, reaching the summit in a burst of glory. They held each other tightly until the tide of passion receded under a gentle rain.

Brandon helped her out of the tub and dried her gently afterward. He wrapped her in the thick terry-cloth robe and carried her into the bedroom. Misty clasped her arms around his neck and rested her head on his shoulder, filled with a pervading happiness.

"You do love me, don't you?" she murmured.

"What do you think?" When she didn't answer immediately, he sat her on the edge of the bed and looked down at her incredulously. "You don't have any doubts, do you?"

"Not a one." She was convinced by his total bewilderment.

"You had me worried for a minute. I don't know what else I can do to convince you."

"Just keep telling me often." She stroked his cheek tenderly.

He turned his head to kiss her fingertips. "That was my intention all along."

It was an enchanted day that would live forever in Misty's memory. The hours slipped by unnoticed as they delighted in everything about each other. Evening came all too soon.

"It's dark outside!" she exclaimed in surprise.

"That's what happens when it gets to be eight o'clock."

"It can't be that late!" she gasped.

"Does that mean the time didn't drag?" he teased.

Misty smiled. "Stop fishing for compliments. I've told you how fantastic you are at least a dozen times."

"How about trying for thirteen?"

"That's unlucky."

"Not for us. We're especially blessed." He took her in his arms and kissed her sweetly. "Nothing can ever come between us."

Maybe not in this fairy-tale place. But they had to go back to the real world.

"I hate to see you go," she said impulsively.

He laughed. "Aren't you coming with me?"

"I meant back to Philadelphia."

Brandon's face sobered. "Why think about that now?"

"Because we don't have very much longer."

"All the more reason to enjoy every minute, sweetheart."

It was the first time he'd admitted their time together was finite. But Brandon still hadn't said anything about the future. After what they'd just shared, Misty felt she had the right to expect some sort of commitment.

"Will we see each other again when we're both back home?" she asked quietly.

"How can you even ask a thing like that?"

"That's no answer, Brandon."

His eyes were tender as he gazed at her, and Misty braced herself to withstand a romantic attempt to divert her. No matter how much she loved him—indeed, *because* of that fact—it was imperative to know where she stood.

Brandon didn't try to be evasive, however. "I can't tell you what the future holds for us, honey. I wish I could promise we'll live happily ever after. God knows that's what I hope will happen. But it isn't that simple. There are pressures on both of us. Other people are involved."

"Sophia?"

"Yes, Sophia, for one." His voice was flat as he agreed.

"She wouldn't stand in the way of our happiness, once she understood."

He hesitated. "Even if I'm wrong—and I pray that I am!—there are other considerations."

Did Brandon think she was concerned that he might be disinherited? Didn't he know that didn't matter? He was all she wanted, rich or poor. While she tried to think of a delicate way to bring up the subject of money, he took both of her hands.

"Just promise that you won't stop loving me," he said urgently. "No matter what happens."

"I never could," she answered simply.

His embrace held a hint of desperation. "I wish we could stop the clock."

"But we can't," she said regretfully. "I suppose we should start back."

"We have time yet. Would you prefer to have dinner here or in the city?"

"I'd like to stay here as long as possible," she answered softly.

It was too cool to eat on the terrace, so they had dinner in the intimate dining room, at a table set with crystal and silver, lit by a tall candle. The food was delicious, but neither of them noticed. They were intoxicated, not by the champagne but by each other.

It was late when Brandon walked Misty to her door and left her reluctantly. His kiss was warm on her lips as she went into the suite.

Sophia came out of her bedroom. "Where have you been all this time?" she demanded. "I was beginning to think you weren't coming home."

The shrill tone was completely unlike her aunt. "Brandon told you we'd be late," Misty answered steadily.

Sophia did an abrupt turnaround. "I didn't mean to sound like a shrew, darling. It's just that I was worried about you."

"Why? You've never treated me like a child before. Weren't you the one who advised me to go out and have new experiences?" Misty asked dryly.

"That's what distressed me all the day. The knowledge that I'm responsible."

"And I'll always be grateful to you."

Sophia sank down onto the couch. "I don't suppose there's any point in my trying to talk sense into you."

"Not your kind. Brandon and I are in love." Misty's face was radiant.

"Oh, dear. This is what I was afraid of."

"Why can't you be happy for us?"

"I would be if I thought it was reciprocal. But Brandon has a very smooth line. You're only hearing what you want to hear. *You're* in love. He's just amusing himself."

"How about you, Sophia?" Misty challenged. "Warren has that light in his eyes. Is he only interested in one thing?"

Unaccustomed color stained her aunt's cheeks. "The two men are complete opposites."

"Are you sure you're not kidding yourself?"

"Warren is a mature man," Sophia answered stiffly.

"And mature men never string women along?" Misty asked derisively.

"Of course they do, but Warren is different!"

"I guess you've just proved your own point. Women in love will believe anything."

"My situation has nothing to do with yours."

"Do you expect to see him again after you both leave Rome?"

"Yes." Sophia's answer held confidence.

"Has he said anything definite?" Misty persisted.

"We've just talked generally. Warren has been alone so long that I think he's hesitant about making a commitment. Things happened so fast between us. I suppose he wants to be sure it's not just the romance of Rome."

"If you've gotten this close, he must have discussed his family with you." As Sophia frowned at the question that had caused dissension between them in the past, Misty added hastily, "Grown children might take a dim view of their father finding romance after all this time."

"That's always a possibility," Sophia agreed.

"But you and Warren haven't talked about it?"

Her aunt's laughter had a girlish sound. "We seem to have so many other things to occupy us."

Misty was disturbed to discover that Warren still hadn't told Sophia his real reason for being in Rome. If they'd become as close as she indicated, wouldn't he want to confide in her? If only for moral support? Of course, he might be afraid she'd be turned off by his having a juvenile delinquent for a son—if that's all Robby was.

"I really do want you to like Warren," Sophia was saying urgently.

"I do." It was true, in spite of her ambivalence. Misty smiled. "And I really want you to like Brandon."

"Who could help it?" Sophia looked at her fondly. "Maybe I'm wrong about him. How could any man help falling in love with you?"

The days that followed were joyous, even though they had a bittersweet quality, especially as the week drew to a close.

Misty and Brandon were together constantly, sometimes alone, often as a foursome with Sophia and Warren. If her aunt still had doubts about Brandon, she concealed them well, as Misty hid hers about Warren. No one would have guessed the undercurrents that existed among all four of them. The fact that they genuinely enjoyed each other's company made dissembling easy. Plus the fact that they wanted their suspicions to be unfounded.

One day Brandon suggested going to the races, since Misty was finally becoming sated with sight-seeing. The proposal was heartily endorsed by Sophia and Warren. They were all in high spirits as they gathered in the lobby.

"I wonder if it wouldn't be easier to take a taxi," Brandon remarked, glancing toward the revolving door.

"That's an idea," Warren said. "Why bother with the car?"

Something flickered in Brandon's eyes as they lingered on the entrance. "Will you excuse me for a minute?" he said.

"Where are you going?" Sophia asked.

"I forgot my watch."

"We're not on any schedule," she pointed out.

"You don't really need it unless you planned to time the races," Warren agreed. His smile faded as Brandon looked back at him steadily. "On the other hand, you'd probably be lost without it. That's the way I always feel."

"Exactly. I'll be back in a moment."

A few minutes later Misty said, "As long as there's time, I think I'll go up and get my camera."

"Must you?" Sophia asked despairingly. "If you and Brandon keep riding up and down in the elevator all day, we'll *never* get to the races!"

"It will only take me a second." Misty hurried off in the direction Brandon had taken.

She caught up with him unexpectedly. He was talking to a decidedly shady looking character. The man was young, with unkempt blond hair and seedy clothes. He was definitely not one of the hotel guests. As Misty watched, Brandon gave him some money. The man stashed it away furtively and hurried toward the exit.

Brandon stiffened visibly when he turned and saw her. "What are you doing here?"

"I was going upstairs for my camera." Misty was bewildered by his harsh tone. Until a reason for it occurred to her. She grasped his arm excitedly. "Was that Robby?"

"No such luck." Brandon had recovered his poise. "Just a panhandler."

"In the Eden lobby?"

"The poor devil must have been desperate to come in here." He put an arm around her shoulders and led her to the elevator. "Come on, we'd better hurry. If Sophia misses the first race, we'll really catch it."

Much later Misty had a flash of déjà vu. Had that been a glimpse of gold she'd seen on Brandon's wrist? She dismissed the vague impression. If she'd seen anything, it was undoubtedly a cuff link.

Misty knew nothing about horse racing, but the men assured her that not very many other people did, either.

"Maybe the horses know who's going to win, but nobody else does," Warren assured her.

"They must. Otherwise why would people pore over all those tiny statistics in the racing form?"

"It gives them something to do between races," Brandon replied.

"Look at that divine shade of lavender the jockey on number six is wearing," Sophia exclaimed. "I have to bet on him!"

Warren consulted the program in his hand. "Royal Scandal, ridden by Terry Westcott. Finished out of the money in the last nine starts. Came in dead last in the race before this one. Guido's Choice says: 'Born to lose.' Numero Vincere says: 'Can't do it.' Consensus: 'Don't bet him.'"

"Talk about giving a horse a bad name!" Sophia exclaimed indignantly. "Look at that gorgeous animal! Did you ever see such spirit?" She indicated the black horse that was tossing its head and circling, giving its jockey a bad time.

"That's not spirit; that's fear," Brandon teased. "He's trying to get himself disqualified."

"Go ahead, make jokes. Royal Scandal and I will have the last laugh," she declared.

The race was exciting, even though Sophia's selection was last out of the gate. At first the horses were bunched together, but gradually a few pulled away. The lead seesawed back and forth, with everyone urging on his or her choice.

The crowd stood up at the turn and started shouting at the home stretch. Royal Scandal had moved up to the middle of the pack and now put on a burst of speed. He passed the fourth-place horse, then the third and second.

As the spectators screamed themselves hoarse, he and the front-runner ran neck and neck. With a final effort, Royal Scandal crossed the finish line a winner!

Pandemonium reigned. The noise finally died down, only to swell again when the odds were posted. A winning ticket paid thirty to one.

Warren and Brandon congratulated Sophia with a mixture of amusement and amazement.

"You are one lucky lady," Warren said.

"Not at all," she answered crisply. "I merely recognized Royal Scandal's potential."

"Oh, sure," Brandon joked. "You weren't worried when your horse broke last from the gate."

"Not in the slightest. Westcott is a brilliant jockey. He was merely biding his time, looking for a hole so he could move up on the inside when the other horses faded in the stretch. It was a piece of cake."

Brandon raised an eyebrow. "All that girlish enthusiasm over the jockey's lavender and white silks was just a smoke screen? I've always suspected that you're a very devious woman, Sophia."

"I didn't know you knew that much about racing," Misty said when the men had gone to cash in her ticket.

Sophia grinned mischievously. "I don't, but I had to pretend I knew what I was doing. They'd never have let me forget it if I'd admitted I was just partial to lavender."

They weren't as lucky the rest of the day. The men had a few winners, but Misty struck out repeatedly. By the last race she didn't have much hope, but she doggedly studied the program, looking for an inspiration. It came when she spotted a horse named True Love.

"That one!" she exclaimed happily.

Brandon glanced over to see where she was pointing. A tender expression softened his face. "Yes, darling, you chose a winner."

Warren shook his head. "True Love? He's the favorite. You won't make any money on him."

"I don't care about the money," she answered, gazing into Brandon's eyes.

Misty and the two men were pleasantly relaxed after the eventful day. They were considering a quiet dinner and perhaps a movie, if they could find one with English subtitles. But Sophia had other ideas.

"We can do that anywhere," she protested.

"What did you have in mind?" Warren asked.

"I think a little cocktail party would be nice. I really should pay off a few social obligations, and time is getting scarce."

Warren stared at her incredulously. "How can you get a party together on such short notice?"

"Sophia is the pied piper," Misty observed. "All she has to do to round up a crowd is get on the telephone."

"It isn't that difficult," Sophia said modestly. "There are always people who are at loose ends."

"Or they drop everything to be with you." Warren twined his fingers with hers. "Which is understandable. I didn't know how much fun life could be until I met you."

"What a lovely compliment," she answered softly.

Misty had a feeling that Warren would have said a lot more if he and Sophia had been alone. His obvious affection was reassuring. Her aunt's intuition had been right in this case.

When they returned to the hotel, Sophia left them in the lobby. "I'll be up in a minute," she told Misty. "I want to arrange a couple of things with the concierge."

"Can I do anything to help you?" Warren asked.

"No, you've done enough," she said fondly. "This is my party."

They watched her graceful figure cross the lobby as they waited for the elevator. But Sophia didn't go directly to the concierge's desk. Brandon frowned slightly as he saw her stop to speak to Clark Foster. The blond man seemed to have some kind of grievance. He was speaking rapidly while she made an attempt to soothe him. Just before the elevator doors closed, cutting off their view, they saw Sophia open her purse and hand him something.

Misty was uncomfortably aware of the glance Brandon and Warren exchanged over her head. She knew how Brandon felt about Clark.

"Maybe I should have stayed downstairs to run interference for Sophia." She laughed a little diffidently. "She's incapable of hurting anyone's feelings."

Brandon looked at her impassively. "I'm sure your aunt can take care of herself."

Misty was slightly disappointed in his attitude. Did he expect Sophia to be rude? Brandon didn't need anyone to fight his battles for him. But she certainly wasn't going to get into an argument over a wimp like Clark.

Sophia's impromptu "little" cocktail party grew to impressive proportions. The suite was filled with constantly changing faces. Some people stopped by for just a short time on their way to other engagements, but when they left, their places were taken by a new contingent.

Many of the guests were familiar to Misty by now. She had met them at various places with Sophia, although she couldn't remember all their names. The Dedinis were an exception, as they always would be. The handsome couple arrived with an entourage, the countess spectacularly bejeweled as usual. Misty was amused at the way this normally casual crowd made a point of going over to pay their respects. The Dedinis were definitely the resident social lions.

Her amusement faded when Bootsy put in an appearance. Misty hadn't given a thought to the other woman. Of course Sophia had to invite her, but why couldn't she have been busy? Bootsy had paused in the doorway to scan the room, and it wasn't difficult to guess whom she was looking for.

The voluptuous blonde didn't hesitate once she'd sighted her quarry. She headed straight for Brandon. He was standing with a group of people near the improvised bar that had been set up in a corner. Bootsy didn't bother to greet anyone else. Slipping her arm through Brandon's, she gave him a sultry look and said something that raised one of his eyebrows.

Misty turned away in disgust. She no longer viewed Bootsy as a threat; she just didn't like the other woman. It had nothing to do with Brandon. If they'd met under different circumstances, she still wouldn't have liked her. Bootsy was definitely lacking in class, regardless of her money.

Misty understood why Sophia had to invite her, but why Clark? His inclusion in the guest list was a surprise, but not his behavior. Within a few minutes after arriving, he was busily ingratiating himself with a couple she didn't know.

When Misty found herself alone with her aunt for a moment she said, "Did Clark crash the party?" That would be one explanation.

Sophia sighed. "No, I invited him."

"Why would you do a thing like that?"

"I felt sorry for the poor soul."

"Everybody does."

"That's just the point. It's given the man a persecution complex," Sophia said. "He was terribly upset in the lobby earlier because he couldn't get a seat on the plane to Buenos Aires next Sunday. He was sure the airline was lying about being fully booked."

"Why would they do that? They're in business to sell tickets."

"Exactly. Can you imagine taking it personally?"

"Your invitation seems to have restored his confidence." Misty glanced over at a smiling Clark. "That couple might not appreciate it, but I guess you did a good deed."

He aunt laughed. "I did all of Rome a favor. The manager of the airline is a friend of mine. I gave Clark my card and told him he could use my name to get a reservation out of here." Sophia's attention was caught by some newcomers, and she drifted away.

Misty would have preferred to spend all of her time with Brandon, but she felt an obligation to circulate among the guests. Another thing that kept her away from him was Bootsy. She didn't leave his side. Misty avoided them, but Brandon refused to be ignored.

He caught her hand as she was passing by. "I thought this was supposed to be Sophia's party. You've been playing hostess all evening."

"I was just trying to see that everyone's taken care of." She smiled vaguely in Bootsy's direction. "Can I get you anything?"

Bootsy's eyes narrowed on their clasped hands. "Brandon and I make our own entertainment, don't we, darling?" She turned a brilliant smile on him.

After the briefest glance at Misty, he said, "That's an example of how things can be taken out of context."

"Everybody knows about us," Bootsy said carelessly.

Brandon's jawline tightened. "Perhaps I missed something."

"I'd better see if Sophia needs me," Misty murmured. She could sense a scene building.

"No," he said firmly. "I want you here with me."

Bootsy's face flushed with anger. "Don't you think it's time your little girlfriend learned the truth about us?"

"I've already told her," Brandon replied evenly.

"You're a liar!" Bootsy's voice rose.

"That's just one more of your misconceptions," he answered contemptuously.

Bootsy turned on Misty furiously. "I suppose you think you're pretty clever, stealing Brandon away from me. Well, don't gloat too soon. It's holding him that counts, and a dumb little hick like you doesn't have what it takes!"

People were turning around to stare as Bootsy's tirade gained momentum. Misty was rooted to the spot with embarrassment, not knowing what to do. Countess Dedini did it for her.

She drifted over unobtrusively and said, "If you don't stop having these tantrums, darling, you're going to need a face-lift before you're forty. Temper does terrible things to the cords in your neck."

"I wasn't having a tantrum," Bootsy muttered.

"Then you must be coming down with something. I do think you should go home and get into bed."

Bootsy raised her head defiantly, but her angry reply went unspoken as the countess met her gaze steadily. Bootsy wavered for an instant, then turned and stalked to the door. Even in her uncontrolled state, she realized that challenging Countess Dedini could mean social ostracism.

"Thanks, Anna," Brandon said quietly, as the guests resumed their conversations and the incident was glossed over. "You handled that nicely."

"You couldn't very well do it yourself." She smiled. "Gentlemen have unfair restrictions placed on them."

"Are you okay?" He put his hands on Misty's shoulders and looked at her searchingly. "You didn't let her upset you?"

"If you mean did I believe anything she said, no, I didn't."

The strain on Brandon's face was replaced by an expression of tenderness. He tipped Misty's chin up and kissed her sweetly, not caring who watched.

The older woman's eyes lit with an unaccustomed look of mischief. "I'm tempted to give you the same advice I gave Bootsy."

Brandon grinned as he put his arm around Misty and hugged her close. "Don't think I wouldn't like to take it."

Misty was too happy to be embarrassed. Brandon had made his commitment openly! Now everyone knew how they felt about each other.

Warren joined them a little later. "Nice party." He smiled at Misty.

"I told you Sophia could always draw a crowd," she replied.

"She's remarkably lenient with her guest list," Brandon remarked, a trifle grimly.

"I heard about the little incident," Warren said.

"Someone can always be counted on to drink too much at a cocktail party," Misty said dismissively. She thought that was the best way to handle it.

"I wasn't referring only to Bootsy."

Brandon was gazing across the room at Clark. After Warren followed his direction, the two men exchanged an expressionless look.

Misty suppressed a sigh. One down and one to go. If only Clark would follow Bootsy's example and leave, she could relax and really enjoy herself.

"I didn't realize Sophia was so friendly with Foster," Warren remarked.

"She isn't. I told you what a softy she is," Misty explained.

"So you said." Brandon's voice held a distinct note of cynicism.

Misty didn't want ill feeling to build between Brandon and her aunt. "Sophia only invited him because he was in such a stew about not being able to leave town," she said earnestly.

Brandon's long body tensed. "Where's he going?"

"He wants to go to Buenos Aires."

"Argentina," Brandon said softly. His eyes met Warren's again.

"I thought he was doing the decorating for the big party at the Dedinis' Saturday night," Warren said.

"He is. Clark wanted to leave on Sunday, but there was some hitch over his ticket. He was paranoid until Sophia arranged it for him."

"Your aunt is helping Foster get out of the country?" Brandon demanded.

"That's a strange way of putting it," Misty protested. "She was only doing Clark a favor. She does the same thing for a lot of people."

"I'll just bet she does," Brandon muttered, almost inaudibly.

Misty gave him a troubled look. "I'll admit you have reason to dislike Clark, but Sophia isn't taking sides. She's just a naturally nice person."

Brandon's displeasure vanished as he gazed at her pleading face. "So are you, my little love," he said huskily.

The party went on all evening. The plentiful supply of hot and cold hors d'oeuvres was evidently enough for many people, because they didn't leave to have dinner elsewhere. It was midnight before the last guests left, including Brandon and Warren.

Sophia kicked off her shoes and sank down on the couch, surveying the room appraisingly. Although the hotel waiters had cleared away the food and drinks, the living room had a subtle air of disarray.

"I think it went well," she remarked.

"Everyone had a wonderful time," Misty agreed.

"We even had entertainment. They'll be talking about Bootsy's latest indiscretion for days," Sophia commented dryly.

"I don't know why everybody puts up with her," Misty burst out.

"For all of her money, poor Bootsy is insecure. She never knows if people like her for herself or what she can do for them. You have to feel sorry for someone like that."

"You can carry charity too far," Misty said impatiently. "You aren't responsible for every lame duck in the world."

"I never knew compassion was a vice," Sophia answered mildly.

"It isn't a virtue, either, when it causes misunderstandings with your friends. And your forbearance isn't confined to Bootsy. I wish you hadn't invited Clark tonight."

"What did he do but bore a few people senseless? At a cocktail party the guests expect to meet at least one person like that." Sophia laughed. "It keeps them moving around the room."

"Brandon and Warren don't like him." Misty felt her aunt should know that without being told.

"That's understandable. No one says they have to invite him to *their* parties," Sophia replied coolly.

Misty's frustration showed in her voice. "Why would you risk upsetting someone you care about for someone you don't?"

"Because a principle is involved. I have to approve of myself even if nobody else does."

Misty's annoyance collapsed abruptly. "I don't know what it is about Clark. He's a complete cipher, yet he can start arguments between people who don't care about him one way or another."

Sophia laughed again. "Maybe he's more complex than we thought."

"Or maybe he's a born troublemaker," Misty grumbled. "I'll be glad when he's gone."

"We'll be leaving, too," Sophia reminded her. "We'd better start thinking about whether to go to Paris or London next."

"I'm going home from here," Misty said quietly. She wouldn't have chosen this moment to tell her aunt, but since the subject had come up, she couldn't evade it.

"You're not serious!" When Misty nodded, Sophia said, "But you haven't seen anything yet. This was to be your grand tour."

"I found everything you promised me," Misty answered softly.

"I don't understand. You're talking about Brandon, of course, but if he means that much to you, why would you consider leaving?"

"He's returning home, too."

"Are you sure?" Sophia looked at her doubtfully. "I can hardly believe that."

"I'm very sure," Misty replied confidently.

"Well, even so, if you two are really in love, he'll wait for you. A few weeks aren't going to make that much difference."

Misty laughed out of sheer joyousness. "Sophia, my beloved aunt, I'm very much afraid that you're getting old."

The other woman's frown changed to a bland expression. "It's late, and we're both tired. Why don't we talk about this tomorrow?"

"I won't change my mind," Misty assured her.

Sophia's eyes were troubled as she looked at her radiant niece. "You never know," she answered somberly.

Chapter Ten

Misty was too keyed up to sleep after her conversation with Sophia. She'd never actually told Brandon that she was going home with him—or at least back to the States. But now that she'd gone on record with Sophia, Misty wanted to get things settled. She also ached to see him alone after being surrounded by people all night.

After waiting a short time to be sure that her aunt wasn't going to come to her room to continue their discussion, Misty slipped quietly out of the hall door.

Brandon had given her a key to his suite. She decided to use it instead of knocking on the door at this late hour and perhaps arousing someone in a nearby room. She let herself in silently. As she was about to call out, the sound of voices coming from the bedroom made her freeze like a startled doe.

Misty relaxed when both of the voices were male. She recognized Warren's baritone. Still, disappointment swamped her. She'd looked forward to having Brandon all to herself. They were constantly being frustrated by other people. She sighed, starting to leave as quietly as she'd entered, when their discussion froze her in her tracks. It was an argument actually.

"You're way off base," Warren was saying heatedly. "Sophia is a vital, charming woman."

"So was Delilah," Brandon answered dryly. "Not to mention Mata Hari."

"The comparison is ridiculous!"

Brandon swore pungently. "You're letting your hormones rule your head."

"How I feel about Sophia personally has nothing to do with it," Warren replied stiffly.

"Of course not." Brandon's voice dripped sarcasm. "You just refuse to face facts for good old friendship's sake."

"You don't have any facts. A chance meeting in a hotel lobby, a casual favor that didn't take any effort. That doesn't add up to guilt."

"How about the timing? And his destination? Argentina doesn't have extradition."

Misty was totally bewildered. What were they talking about? Brandon's reference to Argentina seemed to involve Clark, but in what? And what did any of it have to do with her aunt?

"Even if you're right, it doesn't mean Sophia is in on it. She might be an innocent dupe," Warren was saying.

"Sophia is as sharp as they come. Can you see her being taken in by a con artist?"

"If we're correct, Foster is a master criminal, not a petty thief. He could easily be using her."

"I might go along with you if she wasn't pulling her own scam."

"It's not against the law to pretend you have money," Warren protested.

"No, but financing your life-style by lifting other people's property *is*. She has the perfect setup. Who would be in a better position to rip off the idle rich than one of their supposed members?"

Misty had to stop herself from crying out. The shock of discovering they suspected Sophia of being a jewel thief was almost equaled by her disillusion with Brandon. He had betrayed her confidence! He'd twisted the information she'd given him and was using it to blacken her aunt's reputation.

"All of this is supposition." Warren's uncertain tone indicated he was wavering, and his next words proved it. "I'd hate to think you were right."

"How do you think *I* feel?" Brandon asked roughly. "Do you know what this will do to Misty?"

"Have you ever considered that she might be in on it, too?"

"You're out of your mind!"

Warren laughed bitterly. "Now whose hormones are talking?"

"We won't get anywhere fighting among ourselves." Brandon's voice had a hard edge. "May I remind you that there is a great deal of money at stake? You may be willing to blow it, but I'm not."

Warren sighed heavily. "No, I can't do that."

"So we'll proceed according to plan. And I swear, Warren, if you do anything to foul this up..." Brandon's unfinished sentence carried an undertone of menace.

"I won't." Warren sounded defeated. "I'm not in any position to."

"Just remember that."

The noise of a chair being pushed back galvanized Misty. She had been frozen to the spot, rigid with shock and misery. Now a quiver of fear ran through her. These men weren't the urbane gentlemen she'd supposed. They mustn't find her here!

She ran back to her own room with a pounding heart. In the safety of her bedroom, Misty faced the wreck of her dreams. How could she have been so wrong about Brandon? How could *he* have been so tender, so loving, when it was all a lie? He'd never loved her; it was just a means of getting at Sophia for some reason.

Misty suddenly realized that her aunt's romantic expectations were over, too. It didn't give her any satisfaction to know her warnings about Warren had been correct. Sophia had to be told right now. Something this important couldn't wait.

Her aunt was reading in bed. She looked up with a smile. "What's wrong, pet? Can't you sleep?"

Misty took a deep breath. "I have something to tell you."

"What is it?" Sophia asked when she couldn't go on. "You look so serious."

Misty plunged in grimly because there was no easy way to break the news. "Warren and Brandon are saying hateful things about you. They think you're the jewel thief that's been victimizing the continent."

Sophia stared at her in astonishment. "Do you feel all right? You're terribly pale. I think I'd better call the doctor."

"You have to listen to me! Everything I'm saying is true. I heard them with my own ears!"

"What do you think you heard?"

"I don't *think*; I *know*!"

Misty poured out the whole story, not sparing Brandon in the telling. Her anguish was evident, but she repeated every damning word.

Sophia listened quietly. When Misty finished, she looked thoughtful. "I always felt something about Brandon didn't ring true. He's not the decadent playboy type."

"Is that all you can say? How about Warren? Do you still think he's a big oilman from Texas?"

Sophia sighed. "No, I suppose my intuition got tangled up in my heartstrings."

"He's the lowest of the low—they both are. They used us!"

"The question is, why?"

"Supposedly to save Warren's son, Robby, from prison. That was a lie, too," Misty said bitterly. "I should have realized it when Brandon made me promise not to tell you. I'll never forgive myself." When Sophia looked bewildered, she told her that story, too.

"I wonder who they really are? Police, I suppose. Part of that Interpol network, or whatever they call it."

"You mean they might try to arrest you?" Misty gasped.

"I presume they're waiting to catch me with the goods." Sophia laughed unexpectedly. "How's that for gangster lingo?"

Misty paced the floor angrily. "I can't believe anyone could be that devious. All the time they were wining and dining us, they were really looking for incriminating evidence."

"Well, I suppose a policeman is trained to suspect everyone. Actually, I *would* be a prime candidate. I have entrée everywhere, and I do need the money."

"They should know you well enough to realize you'd never do anything dishonest."

Sophia's face was devoid of expression. "A person who's pushed to the wall can sometimes surprise you."

Misty suddenly remembered Brandon's question, "How well do you know your aunt?" She rejected the insinuation violently. She wouldn't let him poison her mind, in addition to everything else he'd done to her.

"Why are you defending them after the way Warren betrayed you?" she demanded. "He'd stand back and let you go to prison! I heard him tell Brandon that he was with him all the way."

Sophia's eyes were shadowed, but she retained her composure. "I didn't say I was delighted, only that I understood. Warren had a job to do, but I'm sure he's not happy about the methods he used."

"Then why did he? If Clark is also a suspect, he could have leaned on *him* instead of sweet-talking *you*."

Sophia's mouth thinned. "Linking me with Clark is something else. If I *were* the jewel thief, I wouldn't pick an inept clod like him for an accomplice."

"You think they're wrong about him, too?"

"Who knows? Offhand I'd say Clark was too nervous to steal, but I no longer trust my instincts. It could be anyone."

Misty felt trapped in a web of intrigue. "Let's get out of here, Sophia—tomorrow!"

The older woman smiled. "Wouldn't that confirm their dire suspicions?"

"I don't care what they think. I never want to see Brandon again, anyway."

"He probably feels badly about the deception, also," Sophia said gently.

"I can't be as forgiving as you."

"At least don't let disillusionment make you bitter. You had good times together. Try to remember those."

Sophia didn't know just how rapturous those times had been. Brandon had been a masterful yet tender lover, for all his duplicity. Desolation settled like a smothering cloud over Misty at the realization that it was all over.

"I want to leave here," she said urgently.

"We will, after the Dedini party. It's only a couple of more days."

"It's just another party. Why can't we go *now*?"

"Because the Dedinis are expecting us, and we don't have a valid reason for disappointing them. We will both hold up our heads and survive this," Sophia said evenly.

Misty realized that her aunt was more deeply hurt than she was admitting. "I'm sorry," she murmured. "I almost wish I hadn't found out."

"Neither of us would want to live in a fool's paradise." Sophia smiled tenderly at her niece's wistful face. "Get some sleep, darling. I can't promise that things will look better in the morning, but life usually compensates for the manure it dumps by producing some flowers eventually."

Misty went to bed, but she couldn't sleep. She reviewed every moment of her relationship with Brandon, trying to find clues that should have alerted her to his deceit. In retrospect they were plentiful, but he'd so beguiled her that she hadn't noticed.

It was dawn before she finally fell into an exhausted sleep. When the telephone woke her at nine o'clock, she picked it up without being fully awake.

"Time to get out of bed, sleepyhead. Unless you'd like me to come over and join you." Brandon's voice held a husky, teasing note.

As her head cleared, Misty was filled with cold fury. "Not now or at any other time!"

"Is this the way you wake up in the morning? My little kitten sounds like a grumpy tiger." He chuckled, not realizing she was serious.

She hung up without answering. When the phone rang a moment later she picked it up with fire in her eyes. "I want you to stop calling me! Is that clear?"

"What's this all about, Misty?" Brandon sounded puzzled. "What have I done?"

"Just about every dirty trick ever invented," she answered grimly. "I know all about you and Warren."

"What do you mean?" he asked warily.

"Exactly what I said. You two are beneath contempt. If that's the only way you could get information, you should be in another line of work."

Misty banged down the receiver and glared at the phone balefully, waiting for it to ring again. When it didn't, she was almost sorry. She'd thought of a few more grievances to air.

Brandon gave her the chance. He banged authoritatively on the bedroom door in a matter of minutes.

Misty considered not answering it, but she knew he wouldn't give up. Her cheeks were pink with anger as she flung open the door.

"What the hell is going on?" he demanded, striding into the room.

"You have a lot of nerve coming here," she raged. "I should think you'd be ashamed to face me!"

"Will you tell me what in God's name happened to put you in this state?"

"How did you expect me to act after you accused my aunt of being a thief?"

A mask descended over his face. "When did I do that?"

"Don't bother thinking up a clever lie. I was in your suite last night. I heard you and Warren talking."

His hands bit into her arms. "Did you tell Sophia this?"

"Of course I told her." She shook off his restraint.

"What did she say?" His lithe body was tense.

"She promised not to steal anything else," Misty replied sarcastically. "How could you even think such a thing? Sophia is the most forthright, open person in the whole world."

Brandon looked uncomfortable. "I know how you feel, darling, but—"

"Don't ever call me that again!" Misty flared. "I don't want to be reminded of what a fool I've been."

"I was afraid you'd take it like this," he muttered, jamming his hands into his pockets.

"You gave me the biggest snow job of the century, and I fell for it! All that garbage about saving poor, misguided Robby from a life of crime. That was a lie, too, wasn't it?"

"Yes."

"A really inspired story, considering you improvised it on the spur of the moment. You and Warren must have had a good laugh at how gullible I was," she said bitterly.

"You're wrong," he answered quietly. "I never got any pleasure out of deceiving you."

"That's rather insulting, considering the fact that you only made love to me *after* I got an inkling of what was going on."

"You can't imagine one thing had anything to do with the other!"

Misty's anger collapsed into sheer misery. "How could you do it, Brandon? I was naïve enough to believe anything you told me. But you had to make sure, didn't you?"

"I love you, Misty," he said urgently. "No matter what else you think about me, you have to believe that."

"You never give up, do you? But why bother? I can't help you anymore."

"I never tried to get information out of you. Be fair, Misty," he pleaded. "You told me about Sophia's financial status. I didn't ask you."

"You didn't tell me she was under suspicion, either. Do you honestly believe she's capable of stealing?"

The taut skin over Brandon's high cheekbones gave his face a pitiless expression. "Anyone is capable of anything under certain circumstances."

That was, in essence, what Sophia had said. The two shared a lot of the same traits. Underneath their charm and elegance was an indomitable will. They could and would do whatever was necessary to survive. Misty was appalled at where her thoughts were leading. No matter what Brandon said, Sophia was innocent.

"We have nothing further to discuss," she said stiffly. "Please go."

"We can't let it end like this." A nerve throbbed in his temple. "You can't just ignore the way we feel about each other."

The potent attraction that existed between them was almost tangible. Even now when Misty wanted to feel only loathing, every masculine inch of him mocked her resolve.

She turned her back. "The only person I care about is Sophia."

"I didn't want to hurt your aunt, honey. I'm very fond of Sophia. In fact, I'm relieved that things turned out this way."

Misty whirled around to face him again. "What do you mean?"

"There's no evidence against her at this point." Brandon hesitated. "If she, uh, focuses her energies in a different direction in the future—"

"You mean if she stops stealing," Misty interrupted angrily. "You're really incredible!"

"Face the facts, Misty. She could go to prison," he said sternly. "In spite of what you think, I don't want that to happen."

"But you wouldn't lift a finger to stop it."

"I would if I could, but too many people are involved now."

"This is insane! I'm talking about my own aunt as though I believed your lies. You're very clever at twisting things around, but I'm not a starry-eyed innocent anymore. For all I know, *you* could be the cat burglar and this is all a smoke screen. How do I know you're really a policeman?"

A startled look crossed Brandon's face. "I never told you that."

"Then who— No, don't tell me! It wouldn't be the truth, anyway." She put her hands over her ears. "Just leave me alone, Brandon. Get out of my life!"

"If that's the way you want it," he said quietly. Regret darkened his eyes as he stared at her taut figure. "I'm sorry it had to end this way."

He waited, but when she didn't answer, he walked silently to the door.

The finality of their break was like a leaden weight pressing on Misty's chest. It crushed all hope that somehow there was an explanation that would set everything right. No miracle was going to occur. The idyll was over.

Sophia was sitting at the desk writing notes when Misty wandered into the living room some time later. She glanced up and smiled, as though a door hadn't just slammed in both their faces.

"Good morning, pet. Coffee's on the table over there. If you'd like breakfast, ring room service."

"No thanks, coffee is all I want." Misty walked over and poured herself a cup.

"What shall we do today?" her aunt asked brightly. "Varensi is showing his new fall collection. That sounds like fun."

"Not to me." Misty stared somberly into her coffee.

"Nonsense. You know that old saying—when the going gets tough, the tough go shopping."

Sophia's manner and appearance were the same as always. The faint smudges under her eyes that makeup couldn't quite conceal were the only evidence of the sleepless night she must have spent.

Misty admired her aunt's unquenchable spirit. She attempted a smile. "I hope you know that slogan was invented by the retailers of the world."

"It's one of the few catch phrases that make sense, though," Sophia answered dryly.

"What time is the fashion show?"

"Not till this afternoon."

Misty wondered how she was going to get through the morning. She stood up restlessly. "Maybe I'll go out for a walk or something."

"That's a good idea."

"Would you like to join me?"

"No thanks. I have letters to write." Sophia smiled faintly. "We all cope in our own way."

"Brandon came to see me this morning," Misty said abruptly.

"I thought I heard voices."

"No doubt," Misty answered grimly.

"I gather you didn't accept his apology."

"He didn't make one!" Misty looked at her aunt sharply. "Don't tell me you let Warren talk *you* around?"

"I haven't heard from Warren," Sophia said quietly. "I imagine Brandon told him about the new developments."

Misty's eyes flashed with indignation. "That coward! He could still call and give you the opportunity to tell him what you think of him."

"Did you feel better after you told Brandon?"

"It's the principle of the thing," Misty muttered.

"I'd prefer to leave things as they are. Warren was a delightful companion. I'll remember him fondly."

The finality in her aunt's voice told Misty it was pointless to argue, but she stubbornly got in the last word. "I still think he owes you something."

The telephone shrilled suddenly, causing them both to stiffen. Sophia recovered immediately. Her face was composed as she picked up the receiver.

Any remaining tension was dispelled as she said, "Yes, she's here, Duane."

Misty took the phone reluctantly. "Hello, Duane."

"I'll give you one more chance to accept my invitation for a lavish night on the town," he said without preamble.

"My aunt might have plans," Misty answered lamely.

"You can do better than that. If you don't want to go out with me, say so like a man."

Maybe honesty *was* the best policy. "I don't want to go out with you, Duane," she said quietly. "It's nothing personal. I'm just not feeling too cheerful at the moment."

"That's better. See how easy it was? Now, what time shall I pick you up this evening?"

"Didn't you hear what I said?"

"Certainly. I have twenty-twenty hearing. It's my comprehension that's defective."

"I really wouldn't be very good company."

"You might surprise yourself and have a smashing time," he coaxed. "I'll do my Cary Grant imitation."

Misty smiled in spite of herself. "Not 'Judy, Judy, Judy'?"

"Has someone been stealing my material?" he asked indignantly. "Well, no matter. I'll think of something else. Is it a date?"

Duane's lightheartedness had a knack of cheering her up. Maybe she wouldn't have the smashing time he predicted, but going out with him made a lot more sense than staying home and listening to her heart break.

"It's a date," she answered.

Misty had a better time than she'd expected, mainly because she tried very hard. It wasn't the sort of evening she ordinarily would have preferred, but that night it was just what she needed.

Duane and his crowd were like restless lemmings, always on the move in search of some as yet undiscovered pleasure spot. They traveled an irregular path between discos, nightclubs, jazz joints—anyplace that offered entertainment to their jaded palates.

Misty let herself be swept along in the mindless hedonism. If she laughed loud enough, danced fast enough, the past and future ceased to exist.

The one thing she was afraid of was running into Brandon. All of these people frequented the same spots. At first she tensed at every glimpse of a tall, dark-haired man, every broad-shouldered male seen from a distance. But if Brandon was out partying, too, at least their paths didn't cross.

Duane took it for granted that once he'd made the breakthrough, Misty would spend all her time with him. "Tomorrow I think we'll play tennis," he remarked casually during the evening.

"Are you asking me or telling me?" she inquired.

"Naturally the choice of activity is up to you. As long as you don't pick something gross like bowling."

"What's wrong with bowling?"

"For one thing, the ball is obscenely heavy. I don't lift a *suitcase* that weighs that much!"

"You don't carry your own luggage, period."

"Precisely. So how about a couple of sets of moderately strenuous tennis?"

"Are you sure you don't want to hire someone to play them for you?" she asked dryly.

"Do I detect a note of derision? I'll have you know, young woman, that I was on the tennis team in both prep school and college. I'm a superb athlete, as you can probably tell by my magnificent physique."

"How good are you at losing? I'm a pretty fair tennis player myself."

"You aren't honestly suggesting you might beat me?"

"I'm certainly going to try."

He pretended to look horrified. "You're not one of those competitive females?"

"Are you trying to weasel out?" she taunted.

"Now you've done it! The honor of the Creighton clan is at stake. What shall we play for?"

"The fun of it."

"I have a better idea. How about a weekend in Paris?" he suggested.

"How about lunch?" she countered.

"I couldn't let a woman pay for my lunch."

"And I couldn't let a man take me away for a weekend," she replied evenly.

"Well, we'll think of something."

Misty thought he'd gotten the message, but after the group broke up in the early morning hours, Duane didn't take her back to the hotel.

When he pulled up to the curb in an unfamiliar neighborhood, she objected. "No more, Duane. I don't care how amusing this new spot is, I've had enough."

"You don't know what enticements I have planned," he answered lightly.

"Fifty Beatle look-alikes could be singing 'Sgt. Pepper's Lonely Hearts' Club Band' in Italian, and I still wouldn't be interested. I want to go to bed."

He laughed softly. "Your wish is my command."

Misty suddenly got the picture. "Where are we?" she asked sharply.

"My apartment."

Her first reaction was anger, but she didn't care to make a scene. "You're a little premature," she said coolly. "I don't even kiss on a first date."

"Funny you should mention that," he murmured. "I've been wanting to kiss you all night."

"Take me home, Duane," she said flatly.

"That's not very friendly. Why don't we go up to my apartment for a nightcap? I'll ply you with champagne, and then you'll tear at my clothes and beg me to make love to you."

Misty needn't have worried about the situation getting sticky. Everything was a joke to Duane, even romance. He would make love to her if she permitted it, but it would be purely physical enjoyment for him, no more meaningful than a good dinner or a glass of fine wine.

"You've never cared about anyone, have you?" she asked slowly.

"I could." His voice deepened.

She examined his handsome face intently. "No, I don't think you could."

"Hey, you're not going to get serious on me, are you?"

Misty smiled at the startled note in his voice. It was the first genuine emotion she'd detected. "I will if you don't take me home," she warned.

He relaxed as she slipped back into accepted behavior. "You're passing up a good thing. I validate parking tickets."

"I don't own a car."

"I'll buy you one." When she just looked at him steadily, Duane sighed. "Okay, you win. This is why I never went into sales. Rejection depresses me."

"You'll bounce back," she said cynically. "I have faith in you."

"I'll get even at tennis tomorrow," he remarked as they pulled away from the curb. "I was going to let you win, but no more Mr. Nice Guy."

"Our date is still on?" Misty asked in surprise.

"Now who's trying to weasel out?"

"It isn't that. I just thought you might have changed your mind."

"Because you turned down an offer I didn't expect you to refuse?" He shrugged. "You win some, you lose some. It's nothing to get pushed out of shape about."

That was Duane's whole philosophy of life. Misty envied him. It would be nice not to feel deeply about anything or anybody. Or would it? She'd reached undreamed of heights in the short time she'd known Brandon. The agony she was experiencing now was almost as intense, but maybe in time the pleasure would be worth the pain.

Misty's thoughts were somber as she walked down the hotel corridor next to Duane. Although she'd tried to dissuade him, he'd insisted on accompanying her all the way to her door.

"Aren't you glad I'm here now?" he asked. "These halls are spooky."

"They always dim the lights after midnight. I don't know why."

He laughed. "You're a little naïve, doll face. That's so no one can identify the guys playing musical hotel rooms."

"That can't be the reason. What happens if a biological urge strikes *before* midnight?"

"They risk a confrontation with the hotel detective—and a messy divorce."

"You have a cynical mind."

"And the practicality to go with it. That's why I always carry a pocket flashlight—to avoid stubbed toes on strange hotel room furniture."

"In that case, you won't have any trouble finding your way back to the elevator." They'd reached her door, and Misty took out her key. "Good night, Duane. It was a fun evening."

"Not as much fun as it could still be," he murmured, sliding his arms around her waist.

She held him off with palms flattened against his chest. "I thought we'd settled all that."

"I just realized what it takes to be a good salesman. You have to give samples."

"I'm not interested in the product," she said curtly.

"It's something everyone needs," he coaxed.

His arms tightened, and he captured her mouth. Misty struggled, uttering a low protest, but Duane was too strong for her. She could feel the shifting muscles in his broad shoulders. They reminded her of Brandon's. His kiss was in Brandon's class, too, wholly male and designed to be seductive. But Misty felt nothing but revulsion. She flinched at the contact with Duane's taut body.

He finally released her, reluctantly. "Still not buying?"

"I'm sorry," she mumbled.

Misty was sorrier than he knew. Her total lack of response to a man who was handsome, virile and experienced was frightening. Had Brandon left his mark on her forever?

The remaining days slipped by like grains of sand in an hourglass. Misty kept so busy that she was scarcely aware of what day it was. Time had no meaning, anyway. It was just something to be gotten through until the hurt subsided.

Sophia stopped her one day as she was leaving to meet Duane. "I thought you'd like to know that I've made our reservations for Paris. We leave on Sunday."

Although it was welcome news, Misty was surprised. "The party is Saturday night. Won't we be out until late?"

"Our flight isn't till afternoon. I thought you were anxious to leave Rome."

"I am! I was just concerned about you."

"Don't be. I don't need much sleep." Sophia smiled determinedly. "Besides, I can't wait to show you Paris."

Misty wasn't fooled by her aunt's gallant effort. Sophia wasn't having an easy time of it, either. She gave an answering smile. "It sounds really exciting."

By Saturday Misty was keyed up and restless. Duane had decided to save his energy for the party, after their late night the evening before, so she was left at loose ends.

Sophia had gone to the beauty shop, but Misty intended to wash her own hair. She had very little else to do that day. Packing took up some time, but not enough.

In the late afternoon when the silent suite became oppressive, she decided to take a walk.

The lobby was filled with happy, laughing people. Why couldn't happiness rub off like carbon paper? she wondered. Or did carbon paper even exist anymore in this electronic age? Misty was so absorbed in her somber thoughts that she didn't see Brandon crossing the lobby toward her.

The first inkling she had was when he blocked her path. Her heart began to race so rapidly that she actually felt dizzy. It seemed like an eternity since she'd seen him, yet nothing had changed. Brandon still had the power to make her feel weak.

He gripped her arms, looking at her with concern. "Are you all right?"

His touch was intolerable. She wanted to throw herself into his arms and tell him it didn't matter what he'd done. She had to call up every ounce of willpower to save her self-respect.

Raising her chin, she said coolly, "Of course I'm all right. Why wouldn't I be?"

He stared at her searchingly. "You've lost weight."

Misty already knew that. She'd noticed how enormous her eyes appeared in her pale face. Brandon looked thinner, too, but it was becoming to him. The prominent cheekbones and taut jawline gave him a lean and dangerous look, like a pared down male animal in its prime.

She answered his observation carelessly. "Too many late nights. I hope Paris will be less hectic."

"You're leaving Rome?"

She nodded. "Tomorrow."

Brandon tensed. "Why tomorrow?"

"Why not?"

"Isn't that a rather sudden decision?" he persisted.

"Still in there pitching, aren't you?" Misty asked bitterly. "It must be very frustrating for you that Sophia hasn't stolen anything lately."

"You never understood. I have to talk to you before you go," he said urgently.

"Even if I were willing—which I'm not—there wouldn't be time."

"When does your plane leave?"

"It doesn't matter. This is goodbye, Brandon."

Misty forced herself to meet his gaze steadily. She knew she couldn't risk a private encounter with him. This was the best thing that could have happened, no matter how painful. Their formal farewell left no strings untied.

Brandon was unwilling to accept the fact. "I'll see you tonight at the ball."

"Maybe, and maybe not. With five hundred guests, we'll be lucky to find our host and hostess."

"This isn't the end, Misty," he said quietly. "I have some things to say to you. Whether they make any difference is up to you, but you have to hear them."

"The time for explanations is past. Goodbye, Brandon," she said with more firmness than she felt.

It was an effort to walk away, but she managed it. Misty was unaware of the bleakness in Brandon's eyes as they followed her.

ROBO LESSON ON ROMANCE   229

I couldn't be squeamish once he went into the room where
he was trapped. He'd rather I couldn't run the
risk of getting shot. I did something the way I didn't
know what game in kitchen but. Because there is no
choice at rest.

Chapter Eleven

Misty had shopped with great enthusiasm for a red
dress to wear to the ball. She had been looking forward
to Brandon's reaction when he saw her in it. The short
taffeta gown had a low neckline, big poufs for sleeves and
a bubble skirt. The bare back was underscored by a huge
bow at the waist.

She hadn't even minded the cost when she visualized
the results. Now the dress was just an expensive indul-
gence. She shrugged off the error in judgment. Too many
other mistakes in her life had been more costly.

Despite her indifference toward the evening, Misty
took pains with her appearance. In the back of her mind
was the possibility of seeing Brandon again, but she
didn't admit it. Sophia would expect her to look her best
was the way she rationalized.

Her aunt gave full approval. "You look fantastic,
darling. That gown is a real showstopper."

"I doubt if anyone will notice, since all the women at the party will be wearing the same color."

"None of them will look as divine as you."

Misty smiled. "It's nice to get an unbiased opinion."

"Wait and see. The men will gather like hawks. I think you were wise not to go with Duane."

He had asked to escort her, but the party wouldn't be enough for him. He'd expect to wind up the evening with breakfast at dawn, probably at some distant spot. The hectic activity with Duane had helped her over a bad period, but it was almost over now.

Lights were shining from every room in the Dedini mansion when Misty and Sophia arrived, although the party was being held in the ballroom on the top floor. Their taxi had to wait in line while limousines discharged a steady stream of glittering guests.

The baronial front doors of the villa opened on to a central foyer lit by crystal sconces on the plum-colored, damask-covered walls. A curving marble staircase led to the upper floors, but guests were shown to an elevator for the trip to the top story.

Even after the opulence she'd glimpsed, Misty was unprepared for the spectacle that awaited. The huge ballroom that covered the entire top story was transformed into a lush wilderness, complete with apple trees, grass carpeting on everything but the dance floor, and even a waterfall. It cascaded down from the fifteen-foot ceiling over rocks made of crystal that sparkled like a tower of diamonds piled haphazardly.

"I've never seen anything like this!" Misty gasped. "Look up there! Are those real birds?"

The treetops were alive with white doves and brilliantly colored birds of many varieties. They balanced

like miniature tightrope walkers on the long ropes of orchids that garlanded the branches.

"Clark is really a genius," Sophia agreed.

While they were gazing around, discovering new wonders at every turn, Duane came up behind Misty and put
his arms around her waist.

"Where have you been? I've been standing by the door
so long, five people thought I was the butler," he complained.

"Be careful, you'll crush my bow," she cautioned.

"Never! That's something a Harvard man might do,
not a Princeton grad."

Misty switched her attention back to the exotic setting. "I can't believe Clark did all this."

"Makes you wonder what God could have done if he'd
had money to work with," Duane answered.

"Do you realize those aren't cut flowers? They're actually planted there." Sophia indicated banks of orchids
under the base of the trees.

"They're gorgeous, but somehow I never thought of
the Garden of Eden as being subtropical," Misty remarked.

"Me, either," Duane agreed. "I pictured it as somewhere in upstate New York."

"That's really weird, Duane, even for you," she exclaimed.

"I don't know why. Isn't that where apples come
from? The ones that aren't grown in supermarkets, I
mean."

"Didn't they teach you anything at Princeton?" Misty
asked. "Apples are really found in a cabbage patch."

"Like babies?" He gave her an incredulous stare.
"Don't tell me you still believe those fables they feed to

children? Everybody knows babies come from test tubes."

"And you thought Duane wasn't brainy," Misty said to Sophia.

"Leave me out of this." Sophia laughed, moving away to join some friends.

"Enough of this intellectual conversation," Duane said. "Let's dance."

The dance floor was the only part of the sylvan wonderland that wasn't natural, but even that had been painted green.

"How will they ever get the floor back to normal?" Misty wondered.

"A lot of elbow grease and even more money."

"It seems like a lot of effort for one night," she remarked.

"One night can be very worthwhile." Duane pulled her closer.

Misty's relaxed enjoyment vanished as she was reminded of her last night with Brandon. Was it worth this gnawing emptiness inside? When she remembered his enflaming caresses, the touch of his hands and mouth, the answer should have been clear. But the price had been too high.

"That dress really turns me on," Duane murmured in her ear. "Let's find some quiet place where we can make out."

Misty forced Brandon out of her thoughts. He was a closed chapter in her life. "There *is* no quiet place here," she answered lightly.

"If the real Garden of Eden had been this crowded, Adam and Eve could never have started the human race," he grumbled.

"If it had been this crowded, they wouldn't have had to. Come on, I haven't said hello to our host and hostess yet."

Misty enjoyed dancing, so the evening passed fairly swiftly. She was in great demand and had a constantly changing stream of partners. But Brandon wasn't one of them. Had her prediction about not running into each other been correct? Yet other men found her easily enough. A more likely explanation was that he, too, knew their situation was hopeless.

It was almost midnight before Misty saw Brandon for the first time. He was standing by a window, watching her. She was with a group of people, smiling mechanically while wondering what time it was. Her head was beginning to ache from the noise.

When she turned around and saw him, her heart took a giant leap. Brandon was breathtakingly handsome in his elegant evening clothes. She stood transfixed as he started toward her.

"You look lovely," he said huskily when he reached her side.

"Thank you," she answered in a breathy voice.

"Will you dance with me?"

She moved into his arms wordlessly.

Neither said anything for long minutes. They were both savoring the joy of being together again, their bodies touching, their heartbeats mingling. Misty inhaled the subtle scent of his after-shave and moved her hand surreptitiously over his broad shoulders. He responded by molding her body closer and burying his face in the dark cloud of her hair.

She knew this could only lead to more heartbreak, yet she was powerless to move away. It was Brandon who broke the spell. After brushing his lips across her temple, he lifted his head.

"Let's go out on the balcony," he said in a muted voice.

Misty followed him in a trance, clinging to his hand as he led her through the crowd.

The balcony offered a stunning view of Rome, but for once she was blind to its splendors. Brandon was the main attraction. She shivered, as much from emotion as the chill night air.

He was immediately concerned. "Is it too cold out here for you?"

"No, it's all right."

He took off his dinner jacket and draped it around her shoulders. "Is that better?"

She nodded, pulling it more closely around her to savor the warmth from his body. "Have you been here all evening?" she asked. "I didn't see you until just now."

"I arrived rather late."

"Is Warren around? I didn't see him, either."

"He was with me."

"Well, at least you got here before the party ended. It's something else, isn't it?"

Misty's polite tone masked an inner despair. They were making stilted conversation like a couple of strangers. If she'd had any hope that Brandon had brought her out here to explain away all their problems, that hope died a painful death.

"I'll be glad when it's over," he said harshly.

"Me, too," she answered desolately, knowing they weren't talking about the party.

"Do you still intend to leave tomorrow?"

"Yes."

"What time is your flight?"

"We've been through all that, Brandon."

"If necessary, I'll find you at the airport." His voice was quiet but determined.

Misty wavered. "I suppose you could come to the suite after the party."

"I'd prefer to talk to you alone."

"Do you want me to come to your suite?" She realized it was a dangerous offer, but nothing could have stopped her from making it.

Brandon hesitated. "I really want to talk to you tomorrow."

Misty felt as though he'd dashed cold water in her face. "What you have to say can't be very important if there's no hurry," she said curtly.

He took both her hands and held them tightly. "It's the most important thing in my life!"

"They why don't you want to see me tonight?"

"I'll explain everything tomorrow, darling, I promise."

"Can't you ever tell the truth? Our whole relationship has been filled with evasion and intrigue—and nothing's changed," she declared passionately.

"If you'll just trust me this one time," he pleaded.

"You really have the nerve of a bandit!" She flung his jacket at him and ran inside.

Sophia intercepted her near the door as the band was performing a long drumroll. "I've been looking for you," she said. "It's midnight."

"So that's why my coach turned into a pumpkin," Misty answered bitterly.

"What are you talking about?" But Sophia's attention was distracted. "Let's try to get up closer. Marcello is presenting Anna with her anniversary gift."

The count and countess appeared at the microphone, smiling at their guests.

"Many of you have been at our little anniversary celebrations before," the count said. "For those of you who have not, I would like to explain. Every year at this time I present my dear wife with a token of my esteem, to convey my love and appreciation for all her affection and loyalty throughout these happy years."

As the guests applauded, a servant handed the count a large square velvet box. He opened it and took out a necklace of such magnificence that the assemblage gasped. Even from a distance they could see the huge pear-shaped diamonds dangling from a circlet of only slightly smaller stones.

The jeweled extravagance was worth the fortune the count had paid. When he fastened it around his wife's neck it glittered like a living thing.

Hundreds of voices were raised as the host and hostess kissed with obvious devotion. Misty's throat tightened at the evidence of their love. She could tell it had nothing to do with money. They were rich without it.

A distinguished-looking man joined them at the microphone to talk about his long, happy friendship with the couple. He was followed by many others and by the reading of telegrams from guests who couldn't attend.

After that came lavish entertainment. The stars and entire cast of a current musical performed songs and dances from the show. The guests sat at round tables that had been set up around the dance floor with almost magical speed by an army of waiters. Each table was covered with a white lace cloth topped by a crystal bowl of scarlet roses. After the entertainment, an elaborate supper was served.

"I thought all those marvelous hors d'oeuvres were dinner," Misty remarked to Sophia. Delicious delicacies had been passed all evening.

"They were. This is supper."

Misty raised her eyebrows. "Oysters with caviar, and pheasant under glass?"

Sophia laughed. "Were you expecting a peanut butter and jelly sandwich?"

"Nothing I could have imagined would have approached this." Misty's dazzled eyes watched the waiters bringing in huge layers of flaming baked Alaska.

After supper the music started again, and tireless guests filled the dance floor. The man on Misty's left asked her to dance, but she'd had enough.

After declining, she said to Sophia, "If you don't mind, I'm going to cut out."

"Go ahead, pet. I want to visit with Anna and Marcello for a short time, then I'll probably leave, too."

Misty took a cab back to the hotel. Although the ball had been an experience, her head was throbbing, and she wanted to be alone. The entertainment had distracted her for a time, but reaction was setting in. Unhappiness had returned with a vengeance.

She got undressed and went to bed with a book. Sleep was out of the question. Even if her personal problems hadn't weighed so heavily, the stimulating evening would have kept her awake.

Misty heard Sophia come in sometime later. Her aunt must have taken it for granted that she was asleep, because she didn't come in to review the evening. Misty was just as glad. Her thoughts were no longer on the party. What was Brandon doing now? she wondered. What was the real reason he didn't want to see her?

She tried to push him out of her thoughts and concentrate on the book, but her headache had gotten worse. Aspirin might have helped, but she didn't have any, and she didn't want to wake Sophia.

After a period of indecision, Misty decided to go down to the all-night drugstore in the lobby. That meant getting dressed again, but the alternative was to stay up the rest of the night suffering.

After pulling on a pair of pants and a sweater, Misty very quietly opened the door to the hall. She was startled to see a dark figure moving silently toward the elevator. It was a man dressed all in black, tight jeans and a turtleneck pullover.

Something about the noiseless way he moved, like a stalking predator, made Misty hug the wall to escape detection. Her pulse started to race when she realized the man was Brandon.

Where was he going at this hour, and why was he being so furtive, like someone up to no good? The answer came to her like a thunderclap. Brandon was the cat burglar! He was going to commit a crime!

Everything suddenly fell into place. That was why he didn't want to see her tonight. He had something more important to do. She even knew what it was. Brandon intended to pull off the ultimate theft. He was going to steal the Dedini necklace!

If he were caught, he'd go to prison for years. Didn't he know the count must have taken precautions? Their villa surely had an extensive alarm system.

Misty was taut with apprehension. She had to stop him! No matter how badly he'd treated her, she couldn't bear the thought of him being locked up like an animal. Not Brandon, with his wonderful joy in living. It would kill him!

She ran to the elevator, chafing at the endless delay until it arrived. If only she could catch him before he got away. But the lobby was empty when she finally got downstairs. A sleepy desk clerk was reading a magazine behind the marble counter. He was the only one in sight.

Misty raced out the front door, but Brandon had vanished. She wasted agonizing minutes looking for a cab. The doorman wasn't on duty at this late hour, and not many taxis were cruising. Her nerves were screaming by the time she finally managed to hail a cab.

The Dedini villa was darkened, in contrast to its earlier brilliance. Misty paid the taxi driver and started toward the entrance. She hesitated after walking through the grilled gates, wondering what to do next. Brandon would scarcely use the front door. How would she go about finding him?

As she paused uncertainly, a dark figure came out of the shadows. Misty's heart leaped into her throat, even after she recognized Brandon. The subtle difference in him was slightly frightening.

"What in God's name are you doing here?" he demanded.

"I came to stop you from ruining your life. Don't do it, Brandon," she pleaded. "You'll never get away with it."

He swore savagely under his breath. "Why couldn't you have stayed out of this?"

"Because I love you! I don't care what you've done."

"Go home, Misty," he said urgently. "This is no place for you."

"I won't leave without you," she declared.

"I'll explain everything tomorrow. Just get out of here, *now*!"

"Not unless you come with me." She set her jaw stubbornly.

Even in the dim light she could see the frustration on his face. His body was taut as he glanced over his shoulder into the bushes. In the thigh-molding pants and tight jersey he looked like a black panther, uncertain whether to spring or retreat.

At least he was hesitating. Misty pressed her advantage. "Please give it up, Brandon. You've been lucky so far, but you're bound to get caught."

His expression hardened. "I'm sorry, Misty. I hate to do this, but you leave me no choice." Before she could anticipate his intention, Brandon said, "Take care of her, Warren."

Misty panicked as another dark figure moved out of the bushes. She opened her mouth to scream, but Warren clamped a hand over her mouth and dragged her into the shrubbery. Her wild struggles were ineffective against his superior strength.

"Be quiet," he ordered harshly. "It will all be over in a few minutes."

Misty's body went limp with shock. Was this kind, gentle Warren, the man she'd hoped would someday be her uncle? She no longer knew either of these men. The civilized masks they'd worn were gone. These were hardened criminals who wouldn't hesitate to eliminate anything—or anybody—in their path.

As she waited hopelessly for the final curtain to descend on her own personal tragedy, an indistinct figure sidled through the gate and melted into the bushes across from them. What happened next was an incomprehensible blur.

Two figures struggled briefly before the taller one knocked out the shorter one. The moonlight revealed

Brandon kneeling over a prone body. After tying up the figure on the ground, he dragged it into the darkness.

Misty was frozen with fear. Who had Brandon attacked? And how badly was the person hurt? She renewed her struggles, but Warren merely tightened his grip. There was no help from that quarter. His eyes glittered with satisfaction.

The garden returned to its deceptive quiet, but she could sense tension in the very air. What were they waiting for? Her nerves vibrated at every whisper on the breeze, every muted bird sound. When Warren's arm tightened like a vise around her waist, Misty knew the climax was coming.

A man slunk around the corner of the house, keeping to the shadows as much as possible. When he was forced to cross the grass in order to get to the gate, Brandon sprang with the suddenness of a dangerous animal. The two men locked in a fierce struggle that was all the more deadly because it was silent. Their bodies merged and then parted, as one or the other gained an advantage. Misty couldn't tell who was winning, since they were both about the same height, and both were dressed in black.

Warren had the same trouble. After a tense few moments he released Misty with a harsh command to stay where she was. But by the time he started forward, the fight was over. Brandon was clamping the other man's arms behind his back.

"I got him," he called triumphantly.

"Good work," Warren called back.

Misty was rooted to the spot. The third man was Clark.

His face was twisted with hatred. "What the hell are you doing here, rich boy?"

"The same thing you are." Brandon's voice was steely.

"I don't know what you're talking about," Clark blustered.

"We both know you do, so hand it over."

Clark strained to get free. "You're crazy if you think I'm going to give you a cut," he snarled.

"You're in no position to bargain," Brandon answered. "Get the necklace, Warren."

"Wait a minute!" Clark flinched away as Warren reached into his pocket. "You can't have it! This is *my* heist. I planned the whole thing."

"Good of you to admit it," Warren answered grimly.

After a look at their hard faces, Clark's fury turned to a whine. "Look, guys, there's plenty here for all of us. You're just amateurs. You wouldn't know what to do with a piece this hot. I have the fence all set up. Let's go someplace and talk about a split."

"You've talked enough," Brandon said. "Let's get this over with, Warren."

Misty's blood ran cold as Warren reached into his pocket and brought out a dark object. She heard a click and a peculiar sound.

"You can bring your men in now," he said into a walkie-talkie.

Swarms of policemen descended on the stately garden, shattering the quiet as they milled around. While one of the policemen handcuffed Clark, Brandon led another into the bushes. They returned with the man whom Misty recognized as Dante Passetori, the count she'd seen briefly at Bootsy's party. He was conscious now, and handcuffed like Clark.

After the two had been led away by the police, Warren squeezed Brandon's shoulder. "I have to hand it to you. You're one helluva detective."

"I did my job." Brandon's face was expressionless as he stared at Misty, standing across the path.

Warren glanced at her rigid figure, too. "Maybe now we can both mend our fences," he said gently.

Brandon walked slowly over to her as Warren left them alone. "I'm sorry you had to go through this. I'll take you home," he said quietly.

Misty could only nod her head. Too many things had happened too fast. Brandon led her out to the street and around the corner to where his car was parked.

"I'd like to explain if you're willing to listen," he said as they drove through the deserted streets.

"You *have* to explain! I don't understand any of this. What did Warren mean when he called you a detective? I thought you were the cat burglar!"

"I know." A smile relieved his strained expression.

"What else was I to think when I saw you sneaking out of the hotel? And then when I found you at the Dedini villa as I suspected, and you told Warren to take care of me...." Her voice trembled.

Brandon crushed her fingers in a convulsive grip. "You couldn't have believed I'd let any harm come to you?"

"I almost didn't care," she answered somberly.

"Dear heart, we need to have a long talk."

He pulled up in front of the hotel and left the car in the driveway. Misty was erupting with questions, but she managed to restrain herself until they got upstairs.

Brandon led her to his suite instead of hers. "Warren has a lot of things to say to Sophia. I've kept him on a tight leash up until now, so I'd like to give them the opportunity to work things out in private if you don't mind."

Misty's only concern was getting some answers. As soon as the door closed she said, "Who are you really?"

"I own a detective agency. I've been working for a consortium of insurance companies that have been paying off the losses for the cat burglaries."

"Why didn't you tell me?" she exclaimed.

Brandon hesitated. "I'd spent over a month building up my image as a jet-setter. It seemed less complicated to let you go on thinking that."

"That wasn't the reason," she said bitterly. "You thought Sophia was a criminal—probably me, too."

"Not you, but I'll admit I suspected your aunt. Especially after you told me about her precarious financial position."

"How could you!"

"Be reasonable, honey. She fit the profile. Whoever was pulling off these thefts needed ingenuity, nerve and, above all, entrée into high society. It had to be someone who could get in and out of the best places without questions being asked."

"Can you honestly imagine Sophia breaking into houses in the middle of the night?" Misty asked scornfully.

"No, I realized she would have had to have an accomplice. The night Bootsy's ring was taken, I knew Foster was involved. He danced with her right before I did. My big mistake was in thinking he was too stupid to be the mastermind."

Misty was momentarily distracted. "Did he really take the ring? He must have nerves of steel to have suggested everyone be searched."

"He wasn't in any danger. He didn't have it on him anymore. When you mentioned going into the garden with him and meeting a departing guest, I knew how Clark had gotten rid of the ring. An educated guess tells me they shook hands, or something like that."

"No, the count asked Clark for a match."

Brandon nodded. "I thought so. The problem was, you didn't remember the man's name. That's why I had to spend so much time with Bootsy. I needed to find out the names and background of all the people who were at the party, but I couldn't very well tell her what I was after. I finally zeroed in on Dante Passetori."

"Didn't the fact that he was a count throw you off?"

Brandon smiled. "Not all of the nobility are wealthy. Besides, Passetori has had a few brushes with the law over possession of stolen property. Nothing was ever proven, but the chances were good that he was Foster's fence."

"How could Clark take such a terrible chance? Stealing Bootsy's ring off her finger! That wasn't his usual method of operation."

"In a way you have to feel sorry for the guy. Clark is a really talented decorator. He was good enough to be retained by the elite, but they treated him like some kind of super servant. He decided to retaliate by ripping them off. In his capacity as interior designer, he could go all over the house and locate the safes and alarm systems. Nobody really paid any attention to him."

"He did seem a little bitter about it, but I thought he was just a complainer."

"Bootsy pushed him too far the night of her party. She ridiculed him openly, and something snapped."

Misty's mouth thinned. "I'm not condoning what Clark did, but I can't feel sorry for her."

"You don't have to. I got her ring back."

"How did you do that?"

Brandon shrugged. "I have informants here and there."

She remembered the scruffy looking man he'd met in the lobby, and the money that had changed hands. "Warren's right. You must be a very good detective. Does he work for you?"

"No, he owns one of the insurance companies involved."

"So everything he told Sophia was a lie," Misty said soberly.

"Not everything." Brandon's voice was gentle. "He never wanted to believe she was mixed up in this."

"Too bad you didn't give her the same benefit of a doubt. It wouldn't surprise me if you still think she was Clark's partner."

"You heard him admit he planned the whole thing." Brandon's firm mouth curved contemptuously. "If Foster could lay the blame off on anyone, he'd have been singing like the proverbial canary."

"That's the only thing you believe in, isn't it? Proof. A person's innate goodness means nothing," she declared hotly.

"I'm a detective, Misty. I have to deal in facts, no matter how painful."

"And you don't care how you get them," she flared. "You were even willing to make love to me in order to nail Sophia. I hope it wasn't too much of a hardship," she added witheringly.

"You know that's not true," he answered quietly. "Those nights in my arms must have told you I love you."

She was unwilling to remember those blissful hours. "Was it out of love that you were planning to send my aunt to prison?"

"I wouldn't have done that."

"How gullible do you think I am? I suppose you were in that garden tonight to provide Sophia with an escort back to the hotel!"

A smile softened the austerity of his face. "Something like that—after I relieved her of the necklace."

"I don't understand," Misty said uncertainly.

"I'm not a policeman. My job isn't to catch criminals. All I was hired to do, technically, was recover stolen property and stop the thefts. As I told you, there was no hard evidence against Sophia."

"But you thought she was guilty. If you didn't turn her over to the police, how could you be sure she wouldn't go on stealing?"

His smile widened into a grin. "That was Warren's responsibility. He planned to persuade Sophia to marry him and move back to Philadelphia—which is where he lives, not Texas." Brandon laughed. "She wouldn't have needed to pursue her wicked ways. Warren is rich enough to keep her in the style she's accustomed to."

Misty felt a rush of happiness for her aunt. "He really loves her?"

"Like a star-struck schoolboy."

"It was good of you to go along with his plan." She had to be grateful to him for that.

"Actually, it was my idea. I'm very fond of Sophia," Brandon said warmly. His expression altered as he gazed at her. "I even hoped to be related to her."

Misty was so dazed by this new turn of events that she didn't grasp the meaning of his words. Had she been all wrong about Brandon's motives? He didn't need to make love to her for information he wasn't going to use, anyway. The implications were so dazzling that she could only stare at him, wide-eyed.

When she didn't say anything, Brandon's expression grew bleak. "I realize it doesn't change anything between us, but I hoped you'd think a little more kindly of me."

"I do." A bubble of pure happiness expanded inside her. "I'd like to thank you."

"For what?" he asked harshly. "Misjudging your aunt? Warren was a better judge of character, and he's an amateur."

"You can't help it if your profession makes you suspicious of everyone. Maybe you just need to get closer to normal people."

"I'll drink to that!" Brandon said grimly.

Misty drifted slowly toward him. When they were only inches apart, she gazed up provocatively. "*I'm* normal," she murmured.

He held himself in check with an effort. "I'm not sure I understand."

"Then perhaps I can put it more simply." She linked her arms around his neck and pulled his head down to hers.

Brandon's eyes blazed with joy as he wrapped his arms around her. "My little angel! Do you know what torture it's been, knowing you hated me?"

"I tried, but I couldn't." She framed his face in her palms. "You can't hate someone you love."

Brandon's kiss expressed all his pent-up longing. He muttered tiny endearments, holding her so tightly against his taut body that they were almost fused together. Misty's yearning was as desperate as his. She dug her fingers into his bunched muscles and murmured her own words of love.

"I've missed you every lonely hour since you sent me away," he groaned, covering her neck with burning kisses.

"I'm here now," she whispered, tilting her head back so he could continue his quest.

"I have to touch you to believe it."

Holding her with one arm around her waist, he stripped off her sweater. She trembled as his hand cupped her breast and his lips slid along the top of her bra. When his tongue slipped inside the lacy fabric to search out her sensitive nipple, she arched her back. The warm, wet sensation sent a shock of delight through her entire body.

"You missed me, too, didn't you, darling?" he asked triumphantly.

"Can't you tell?"

Her hands slid under his jersey to caress his smooth bare skin. Brandon's muscles rippled as he shuddered with pleasure at her sensuous touch. When her fingertips slipped inside his waistband, he gripped her hips and urged them against his.

The force of his desire met an answering wildness in Misty. She pushed his jersey higher and fumbled for his belt buckle. In quick, fluid movements Brandon ripped off his pullover and stepped out of his jeans.

Misty was dazzled by the power and beauty of his splendid male form. She stood perfectly still, staring at the lithe body that resembled a Roman gladiator's. The noblemen of ancient times must have looked like this.

But Brandon was very much alive. He undressed her as impatiently as he'd flung off his own clothes. When she was completely nude he ran his hands over her entire body.

"You're so beautiful," he said hoarsely. "What would I ever do without you?"

His kisses scorched a path that began at her throat and trailed erotically over her breasts before seeking out other vulnerable spots. Misty was aroused almost unbearably by his lips and tongue, his seductive caresses.

Her knees gave way, and she sank to the carpet, clutching Brandon for support. He lowered her gently until she was lying beneath him. The glow in his eyes was almost incandescent as he stared down at her passion-filled face.

They lingered on the brink for just an instant. Then Brandon took full possession. His surging power brought waves of sensation that increased in intensity until Misty was spiraling out of control. She arched her back again and again in joyous, wild abandon. The mounting ecstasy climaxed in a throbbing explosion that brought peace to her straining body.

Brandon's whispered words of love provided the final benediction. Their total fulfillment was as strong a bond between them as their passion.

Misty could have stayed in the same spot forever, secure in Brandon's love. When he gathered her in his arms and stood up, she uttered a small sound of protest.

He merely laughed. "It's time to go to bed, sweetheart. We can't spend all night on the living-room floor."

She clasped her arms around his neck and sighed. "I wish we *could* spend the night together."

"We're going to," he assured her.

"Sophia . . ." she said hesitantly.

"Is a very sympathetic woman." Brandon completed her thought. "She'd understand an engaged couple wanting time to themselves."

Misty raised her head to stare at him with sudden excitement. "Are you asking me to marry you?"

"Weren't you listening when I brought up the subject a short while ago?"

She tightened her grip around his neck. "Oh, Brandon, I never dreamed . . . I mean, it's enough just to . . ." She broke off to smother his face in kisses.

He pulled back the covers and got into bed without releasing her. "Can I take that as an acceptance?" he teased. His merriment vanished as he gazed into her lovely face. "I love you, Misty." The quiet words were more convincing than any flowery phrases.

They kissed tenderly and exchanged pledges of love and trust. Misty had never believed life could be this blissful.

"The best part is that everything turned out right for Sophia, too," she said eventually.

"I wouldn't say that was the *best* part, but I'm happy for both of them. From now on, all of her jewelry will be real." Brandon chuckled.

Misty gazed up into his rugged face and repeated something Brandon had said so prophetically to her. "Some things in life are more precious than jewels."

*   *   *   *   *

ATTRACTIVE, SPACE SAVING BOOK RACK

Display your most prized novels on this handsome and sturdy book rack. The hand-rubbed walnut finish will blend into your library decor with quiet elegance, providing a practical organizer for your favorite hard-or soft-covered books.

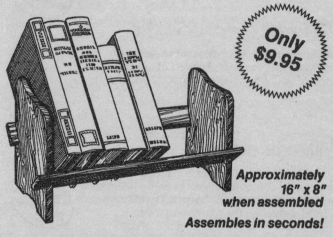

Only $9.95

Approximately 16" x 8" when assembled

Assembles in seconds!

FOUR UNIQUE SERIES FOR EVERY WOMAN YOU ARE...

Silhouette Romance

Love, at its most tender, provocative, emotional...in stories that will make you laugh and cry while bringing you the magic of falling in love.

6 titles per month

Silhouette Special Edition

Sophisticated, substantial and packed with emotion, these powerful novels of life and love will capture your imagination and steal your heart.

6 titles per month

Silhouette Desire

Open the door to romance and passion. Humorous, emotional, compelling—yet always a believable and sensuous story—Silhouette Desire never fails to deliver on the promise of love.

6 titles per month

Silhouette Intimate Moments

Enter a world of excitement, of romance heightened by suspense, adventure and the passions every woman dreams of. Let us sweep you away.

4 titles per month